SPACE TROUBLESHOOTER

Newly accepted as a Special Agent of the star-spanning United Planets organization, Ronny Bronston found that his first assignment was one which had taken the lives of dozens of agents before him: he was to track down a man named Tommy Paine.

"We've been trying to catch him for twenty years," said Ronny's section chief. *"How long before that he was active, we have no way of knowing. It was some time before we became aware that half the revolts, coups d'états and assassinations that occur in the United Planets have his dirty finger stirring around in them."*

"But what motivates him?" Ronny asked. *"What's he get out of all the war and killing he stirs up?"*

"Nobody seems to know. But the best guess is that he's insane—a homicidal maniac on an intergalactic scale. He's dangerous, Ronny, and you've got to get him!"

PLANETARY AGENT X

by

MACK REYNOLDS

WILDSIDE PRESS

PART ONE

I

Aт LEAST HE HAD got far enough to wind up
with a personal interview. It is one thing doing up an appli-
cation and seeing it go onto an endless tape and be fed into
the maw of a machine and then to receive, in a matter of
moments, a neatly printed rejection. It is another to receive
an appointment to be interviewed by a placement officer in
the Commissariat of Interplanetary Affairs, Department of
Personnel. Ronny Bronston was under no illusions. Nine
out of ten men of his age annually made the same applica-
tion. Almost all were annually rejected. Statistically speak-
ing, practically nobody ever got an interplanetary position.
But he had made one step along the path of a lifetime ambition.

PLANETARY AGENT X

He stood at easy attention immediately inside the door. At the desk at the far side of the room the placement officer was going through a sheaf of papers. He looked up and said, "Ronald Bronston? Sit down. You'd like an interplanetary assignment, eh? So would I."

Ronny took the chair. For a moment he tried to appear alert, earnest, ambitious but not *too* ambitious, fearless, devoted to the cause, and indispensable. For a moment. Then he gave it up and looked like Ronny Bronston.

The other looked him over. The personnel official saw a man of averages. In the late twenties. Average height, weight and breadth. Pleasant of face in an average sort of way, but not handsome. Less than sharp in dress, hair inclined to be on the undisciplined side. Brown hair, dark eyes. In a crowd, inconspicuous.

The personnel officer grunted. He pushed a button, said something into his order box. A card slid into the slot and he took it out and stared gloomily at it.

"What're your politics?" he said.

"Politics?" Ronny Bronston said. "I haven't any politics. My father and grandfather before me have been citizens of United Planets. There hasn't been any politics in our family for three generations."

"Family?"

"None."

The other grunted and marked the card. "Racial prejudices?"

"I beg your pardon?"

"Do you have any racial prejudices? Any at all."

"No."

The personnel officer said, "Most people answer that way at first, these days, but some don't at second. For instance, suppose you had to have a blood transfusion. Would you have any objection to it being blood donated by, say, a Negro, a Chinese, or, say, a Jew?"

Ronny ticked it off on his fingers. "One of my great-grandfathers was a French *colon* who married a Moroccan girl. The Moors are a blend of Berber, Arab, Jew and Negro.

6

Another of my great-grandfathers was a Hawaiian. They're largely a blend of Polynesians, Japanese, Chinese and Caucasians, especially Portuguese. Another of my great-grandfathers was Irish, English, and Scotch. He married a girl who was half Latvian, half Russian. Believe me, if I had a blood transfusion from just anybody at all, the blood would feel right at home."

The interviewer snorted, even as he marked the card. "That accounts for three great-grandfathers," he said lightly. "What was the other one?"

Ronny said expressionlessly, "A Texan."

The secretary shrugged and looked at the car again. "Religion?"

"Reformed Agnostic," Ronny said. This one was possibly where he ran into a brick wall. Many of the planets had strong religious beliefs of one sort or another. Some of them had state religions and you either belonged or else.

The personnel officer frowned. "Is there any such church?"

"No. I'm a one-man member. I'm of the opinion that if there are any greater-powers-that-be They're keeping the fact from us. And if that's the way They want it, it's Their business. If and when They want to contact me, then I suppose They'll do it. Meanwhile, I'll wait."

The other said interestedly, "You think that if there is a Higher Power and if It ever wants to get in touch with you, It will?"

"Um-m-m. In Its own good time. Sort of a *don't call Me* thing, *I'll call you*."

The personnel officer said, "There have been a few revealed religions, you know."

"So they said, so they said. None of them have made much sense to me. If a Super-Power wanted to contact man, it seems unlikely to me that it'd be all wrapped up in a lot of complicated gobbledegook. It would all be very clear indeed."

The personnel officer sighed. He marked the card, stuck it back into the slot in his order box and it disappeared.

He looked up at Ronny Bronston. "All right, that's all."

Ronny came to his feet. "Well, what happened?"

The other grinned at him sourly. "Darned if I know," he said. "By the time you get to the outer office, you'll probably find out." He scratched the end of his nose and said, "I sometimes wonder what I'm doing here."

Ronny thanked him, told him goodbye, and left.

In the outer office a girl looked up from a card she'd just pulled from her own order box. "Ronald Bronston?"

"That's right."

She handed the card to him. "You're to go to the office of Ross Metaxa in the Octagon, Commissariat of Interplanetary Affairs, Department of Justice, Bureau of Investigation, Section G."

In a lifetime spent in first preparing for United Planets employment and then working for the organization, Ronny Bronston had never been in the Octagon Building. He'd seen photographs, Tri-D broadcasts and he'd heard several thousand jokes on various levels from pun to obscenity about getting around in the building, but he'd never been there. For that matter, he'd never been in Greater Washington before, other than a long ago tourist trip. Population Statistics, his department, had its main offices in New Copenhagen.

His card was evidently all that he needed for entry.

At the sixth gate he dismissed his car and let it shoot back into the traffic mess. He went up to one of the guard-guides and presented the card.

The guide inspected it. "Section G of the Bureau of Investigation," he muttered. "Every day, something new. I never heard of it."

"It's probably some outfit in charge of cleaning the heads on space liners," Ronny said unhappily. He'd never heard of it either.

"Well, it's no problem," the guard-guide said. He summoned a three-wheel scooter, fed the coördinates into it from Ronny's card, handed the card back and flipped an easy salute. "You'll soon know."

The scooter slid into the Octagon's hall traffic and proceeded up one corridor, down another, twice taking to ascending ramps. Ronny had read somewhere the total miles of corridors in the Octagon. He hadn't believed the figures at the time, but now he did. He must have traversed several miles before they got to the Department of Justice alone. It was another quarter mile to the Bureau of Investigation.

The scooter eventually came to a halt, waited long enough for Ronny to dismount and then hurried back into the traffic.

He entered the office. A neatly uniformed reception girl with a harassed and cynical eye looked up from her desk. "Ronald Bronston?" she said.

"That's right."

"Where've you been?" She had a snappy cuteness. "The commissioner has been waiting for you. Go through that door and to your left."

Ronny went through that door and to the left. There was another door, inconspicuously lettered ROSS METAXA, COMMISSIONER, SECTION G. Ronny knocked and the door opened.

Ross Metaxa was a man in the middle years, with a sour expression and moist eyes, as though he either drank too much or slept too little. He had been going through a wad of papers, but he looked up as Ronny entered.

"Sit down," he said. "You're Ronald Bronston, eh? What do they call you—Ronny? It says here you've got a sense of humor. That's one of the first requirements in this lunatic department."

Ronny sat down and tried to form some opinions of the other by his appearance. He was reminded of nothing so much as the stereotype city editor you saw in the historical romance Tri-Ds. All that was needed was for Metaxa to start banging on buttons and yelling something about tearing down the front page, whatever that meant.

Metaxa said, "It also says you have some queer hobbies. Judo, small weapons target shooting, mountain climbing—" He looked up from the reports, "Why does anybody climb mountains?"

Ronny said, "Nobody's ever figured it out." That didn't seem to be enough, especially since Ross Metaxa was staring

PLANETARY AGENT X

at him, so he added, "Possibly we keep doing it in hopes that someday somebody'll find out."

Ross Metaxa said sourly, "Not *too* much humor, please. You don't act as though getting this position means much to you."

Ronny said slowly, "I figured out some time ago that every young man on Earth yearns for a job that will send him shuttling from one planet to another. To achieve it they study, they sweat, they make all-out efforts to meet and suck up to anybody they think might help. Finally, when and if they get an interview for one of the few openings, they spruce up in their best clothes, put on their best party manners, present themselves as the sincere, high I.Q., ambitious young men that they are—and then flunk their chance. I decided I might as well be what I am."

Ross Metaxa looked at him. "O.K.," he said finally. "We'll give you a try."

Ronny said blankly, "You mean I've got the job?"

"That's right."

"I'll be damned."

"Probably," Metaxa said. He yawned. "Do you know what Section G handles?"

"Well, no, but as for me, just so I get off Earth and see some of the galaxy."

Metaxa had been sitting with his heels on his desk. Now he put them down and reached a hand into a drawer, to emerge with a brown bottle and two glasses. "Do you drink?" he said.

"Of course."

"Even during working hours?" Metaxa scowled.

"When occasion calls."

"Good," Metaxa said. He poured two drinks. "You'll get your fill of seeing the galaxy," he said. "Not that there's much to see. Men can settle only Earth-type planets, and after you've seen a couple of hundred you've seen them all."

Ronny sipped at his drink, then blinked reproachfully down into the glass.

10

Metaxa said, "Good, eh? A kind of tequila they make on Deneb Eight. Bunch of Mexicans settled there."

"What," said Ronny hoarsely, "do they make it out of?"

"Lord only knows," Metaxa said. "To get back to Section G: We're Interplanetary Security. In short, Department Cloak and Dagger. Would you be willing to die for the United Planets, Bronston?"

That curve had come too fast. Ronny blinked again. "Only in emergency," he said. "Who'd want to kill me?"

Metaxa poured another drink. "Many of the people you'll be working with," he said.

"Well, *why?* What will I be doing?"

"You'll be representing United Planets," Metaxa explained. "Representing United Planets in cases where the local situation is such that the folks you're working among will be teed off at the organization."

"Well, why are they members if they don't like the UP?"

"That's a good question," Metaxa said. He yawned. "I guess I'll have to go into my speech." He finished his drink. "Now, shut up till I give you some background. You're probably full of a lot of nonsense you picked up in school."

Ronny shut up. He'd expected more of an air of dedication in the Octagon, particularly in such ethereal departments as that of Interplanetary Justice; however, he was a member now and not adverse to picking up some sophistication beyond the ken of the Earth-bound employees of UP.

The other's voice took on a faraway, slightly bored tone. "It seems that most of the times man gets a really big idea, he goes off half cocked. Just one example. Remember when the ancient Hellenes exploded into the Mediterranean? A score of different city-states began sending out colonies, which in turn sprouted colonies of their own. Take Syracuse, on Sicily. Hardly was she established than, bingo, she sent off colonies to Southern Italy, and they in turn to Southern France, Corsica, the Balearics. Greeks were exploding all over the place, largely without adequate plans, without rhyme or reason. Take Alexander. Roamed off all the way to

11

India, founding cities and colonies of Greeks all along the way."

The older man shifted in his chair. "You wonder what I'm getting at, eh? Well, much the same thing is happening in man's explosion into space, now that he has the ability to leave the solar system behind. Dashing off half cocked, in all directions. He's flowing out over this section of the galaxy without plan, without rhyme or reason." He paused, frowning. "I take that last back. He has reasons, all right—some of the screwiest. Religious reasons, racial reasons, idealistic reasons, political reasons, altruistic reasons and mercenary reasons.

"Inadequate ships, manned by small numbers of inadequate people, setting out to find their own planets, to establish themselves on one of the numberless uninhabited worlds that offer themselves to colonization and exploitation."

Ronny cleared his throat. "Well, isn't that a good thing, sir?"

Ross Metaxa looked at him and grunted. "What difference does it make if it's good or not? It's happening. We're spreading our race out over tens of hundreds of new worlds in the most haphazard fashion. As a result, we of United Planets now have a chaotic mishmash on our hands. How we manage to keep as many planets in the organization as we do sometimes baffles me. I suppose most of them are afraid to drop out, conscious of the protection UP gives against each other."

He picked up a report. "Here's Monet, originally colonized by a bunch of painters, writers, musicians and such. They had dreams of starting a new race"—Metaxa snorted —"with everybody artists. They were all so impractical that they even managed to crash their ship on landing. For three hundred years they were uncontacted. What did they have in the way of government by that time? A military theocracy, something like the Aztecs of Pre-Conquest Mexico. A matriarchy, at that. And what's their religion based on? That of ancient Phoenicia, including plenty of human sacrifice to good old Moloch. What can United Planets do about it, now that they've become a member? Work away very delicately, trying to get them to at least eliminate the child sacrifice phase of their culture. Will they do it? Hell, no, not if they can help it. The Head Priestess and her clique are afraid that if they don't have the threat of sacrifice to hold over the people, they'll be overthrown."

Ronny was surprised. "I'd never heard of a member planet like that. Monet?"

Metaxa sighed. "No, of course not. You've got a lot to learn, Ronny, my lad. First of all, what're Articles One and Two of the United Planets Charter?"

That was easy. Ronny recited, "Article One: *The United Planets organization shall take no steps to interfere with the internal political, socio-economic, or religious institutions of its member planets.* Article Two: *No member planet of United Planets shall interfere with the internal political, socio-economic or religious institutions of any other member planet.*" He looked at the department head. "But what's that got to do with the fact that I was unfamiliar with even the existence of Monet?"

"Suppose one of the advanced planets, or even Earth itself," Metaxa growled, "openly discussed in magazines, on newscasts, or wherever, the religious system of Monet. A howl would go up among the liberals, the progressives, the do-gooders. And the howl would be heard on the other advanced planets. Eventually, the citizen in the street on Monet would hear about it and be affected. And before you knew it, a howl would go up from Monet's government. Why? Because the other planets would be interfering with her internal affairs, simply by discussing them."

"So what you mean is," Ronny said, "part of our job is to keep information about Monet's government and religion from being discussed at all on other member planets."

"That's right," Metaxa nodded. "And that's just one of our dirty little jobs. One of many. Section G, believe me, gets them all. Which brings us to your first assignment."

Ronny inched forward in his chair. "It takes me into space?"

13

"It takes you into space, all right," Metaxa snorted. "At least it will after a few months of indoctrination. I'm sending you out after a legend, Ronny. You're fresh, so possibly you'll get some ideas older men in the game haven't thought of."

"A legend?"

"I'm sending you to look for Tommy Paine. Some members of the department don't think he exists. I do."

"Tommy Paine?"

"A pseudonym that somebody hung on him way back before even my memory in this Section. Did you ever hear of Thomas Paine in American history?"

"He wrote a pamphlet during the Revolutionary War, didn't he?"

Metaxa nodded. "*Common Sense.* But he was more than that. He was born in England but went to America as a young man, and his writings probably did as much as anything to put over the revolt against the British. But that wasn't enough. When that revolution was successful he went back to England and tried to start one there. The government almost caught him, but he escaped and got to France, where he participated in the French Revolution."

"He seemed to get around," Ronny Bronston said.

"And so does this namesake of his. We've been trying to catch up with him for some twenty years. How long before that he was active, we have no way of knowing. It was some time before we became aware of the fact that half the revolts, rebellions, revolutions and such that occur in the United Planets have his dirty finger stirring around in them."

"But you said some department members don't believe in his existence."

Metaxa grunted. "They're working on the theory that no one man could do all that Tommy Paine has laid to him. Possibly it's true that he sometimes gets the blame for accomplishments not his. Or, for that matter, possibly he's more than one person. I don't know."

"Well," Ronny said hesitantly, "what's an example of his activity?"

Metaxa picked up another report from the confusion of his desk. "Here's one only a month old. Dictator on the planet Megas. Kidnapped and forced to resign. There's still confusion, but it looks as though a new type of government will be formed now."

"But how do they know it wasn't just some dissatisfied citizens of Megas?"

"It seems as though the kidnap vehicle was an old fashioned Earth-type helicopter. There were no such on Megas. So Section G suspects it's a possible Tommy Paine case. We could be wrong, of course. That's why I say the man's in the way of being a legend. Perhaps the others are right and he doesn't even exist. I think he does—and if so, it's our job to get him and put him out of circulation."

Ronny said slowly, "But why would that come under our jurisdiction? It seems to me that it would be up to the police of whatever planet he was on."

Ross Metaxa looked thoughfully at his brown bottle, shook his head and returned it to its drawer. He looked at a desk watch. "Don't read into the United Planets organization more than there is. It's a fragile institution with practically no independent powers to wield. Every member planet is jealous of its prerogatives, which is understandable. It's no mistake that Articles One and Two are the basic foundations of the Charter. No member planet wants to be interfered with by any other or by United Planets as an organization. They want to be left alone.

"Within our ranks we have planets with every religion known to man throughout the ages. Everything ranging from primitive animism to the most advanced philosophic ethic. We have every political system ever dreamed of, and every socio-economic system. It can all be blamed on the crackpot manner in which we're colonizing. Any minority, no matter how small—religious, political, racial, or whatever—if it can collect the funds to buy or rent a spacecraft, can dash off on its own, find a new Earth-type planet and set up in business.

"Fine. One of the prime jobs of Section G is to carry out,

to enforce, Articles One and Two of the Charter. A planet with Buddhism as its state religion doesn't want some die-hard Baptist missionary stirring up controversy. A planet with a feudalistic socio-economic system doesn't want some hotshot interplanetary businessman coming in with some big deal that would eventually cause the feudalistic nobility to be tossed onto the ash heap. A planet with a dictatorship doesn't want subversives from some democracy trying to undermine their institutions—and vice versa."

"And it's our job to enforce all this, eh?" Ronny said.

"That's right," Metaxa told him sourly. "It's not always the nicest job in the system. However, if you believe in United Planets, an organization attempting to coördinate, in such a manner as it can, the efforts of its member planets, for the betterment of all, then you must accept Section G and Interplanetary Security."

Ronny Bronston thought about it.

Metaxa added, "That's why one of the requirements of this job is that you yourself be a citizen of United Planets, rather than of any individual planet, have no religious affiliations, no political beliefs, and no racial prejudices. You've got to be able to stand aloof."

"Yeah," Ronny said thoughtfully.

Ross Metaxa looked at his watch again and sighed wearily. "I'll turn you over to one of my assistants," he said. "I'll see you again, though, before you leave."

"Before I leave?" Ronny said, coming to his feet. "But where do I start looking for this Tommy Paine?"

"How the hell would I know?" Ross Metaxa growled.

II

IN THE OUTER OFFICE, Ronny said to the receptionist, "Commissioner Metaxa said for me to get in touch with Sid Jakes."

She said, "I'm Irene Kasansky. Are you with us?"

Ronny said, "I beg your pardon?"

She said impatiently, "Are you going to be with the Sec-

tion? If you are, I've got to clear you with your old job. You
were in statistics over in New Copenhagen, weren't you?"

Somehow it seemed far away now, the job he'd held for
more than five years. "Oh, yes," he said. "Yes, Commissioner
Metaxa has given me an appointment."

She looked up at him. "Probably to look for Tommy Paine."

He was taken aback. "That's right. How did you know?"

"There was talk. This Section is pretty well integrated."
She grimaced, but on her it looked good. "One big happy
family. High interdepartmental morale. That sort of nonsense." She flicked some switches. "You'll find Supervisor
Jakes through that door, one to your left, two to your right."

He could have asked one *what* to his left and two *what*
to his right, but evidently Irene Kasansky thought he had
enough information to get him to his destination. She'd gone
back to her work.

It was one turn to his left and two turns to his right. The
door was lettered simply SIDNEY JAKES. He knocked and a
voice shouted happily, "It's open. It's always open."

Supervisor Jakes was as informal as his superior. His attire
was on the happy-go-lucky side, more suited for sports wear
than a fairly high ranking job in the ultra-staid Octagon.

He couldn't have been much older than Ronny Bronston,
but he had a nervous vitality about him that would have
worn out the other in a few hours. He jumped up and shook
hands. "You must be Bronston. Call me Sid." He waved a
hand at a typed report he'd been reading. "Now I've seen
them all. They've just applied for entry to United Planets.
Republic. What a name, eh?"

"What?" Ronny said.

"Sit down, sit down." He rushed Ronny to a chair, saw
him seated, returned to the desk and flicked an order box
switch. "Irene," he said, "do up a badge for Ronny, will
you? You've got his code, haven't you? Good. Send it over.
Bronze, of course."

Sid Jakes turned back to Ronny and grinned at him. He
motioned to the report again. "What a name for a planet.
Republic. Bunch of screwballs, again. Out in the vicinity of

17

Sirius. Based their system on Plato's *Republic*. Have to go the whole way. Don't even speak Basic. Certainly not. They speak Ancient Greek. That's going to be a neat trick, finding interpreters. How'd you like the Old Man?"

Ronny said, dazed at the conversational barrage, "Old Man? Oh, you mean Commissioner Metaxa."

"Sure, sure," Sid grinned, perching himself on the edge of the desk. "Did he give you that drink of tequila during working hours routine? He'd like to poison every new agent we get. What a character."

The grin was infectious. Ronny said carefully, "Well, I did think his method of hiring a new man was a little—cavalier."

"Cavalier, yet," Sid Jakes chortled. "Look, don't get the Old Man wrong. He knows what he's doing."

"But he took me on after only two or three minutes conversation."

Jakes cocked his head to one side. "Oh? You think so? When did you first apply for interplanetary assignment, Ronny?"

"I don't know, about three years ago."

Jakes nodded. "Well, depend on it, you've been under observation for that length of time. At any one period, Section G is investigating possibly a thousand potential agents. We need men but qualifications are high."

He hopped down from his position, sped around to the other side of the desk and lowered himself into his chair. "Don't get the wrong idea, though. You're not in. You're on probation. Whatever the assignment the Old Man gave you, you've got to carry it out successfully before you're full fledged." He flicked the order-box switch and said, "Irene, where the devil's Ronny's badge?"

Ronny Bronston heard the office girl's voice answer snappishly.

"All right, all right," Jakes said. "I love you, too. Send it in when it comes." He turned to Ronny. "What *is* your assignment?"

"He wants me to go looking for some firebrand nick-

18

named Tommy Paine. I'm supposed to arrest him. The commissioner said you'd give me details."

Sid Jakes' face went serious. He puckered up his lips. "Wow, that'll be a neat trick to pull off," he said. He flicked the order-box switch again. Irene's voice snapped something before he could say anything and Sid Jakes grinned and said, "O.K., O.K., darling, but if this is the way you're going to be I won't marry you. Then what will the children say? Besides, that's not what I called about. Have ballistics do up a model H gun for Ronny, will you? Be sure it's adjusted to his code."

He flicked off the order-box and turned back to Ronny. "I understand you're familiar with hand guns. It's in this report on you."

Ronny nodded. He was just beginning to adjust to this free-wheeling character. "What will I need a gun for?"

Jakes laughed. "Ye Gods, you babe in the woods. Do you realize this Tommy Paine character has supposedly stirred up a couple of score wars, revolutions and revolts? Not to speak of having laid in his lap two or three dozen assassinations. He's a quick lad with a gun. A regular Nihilist."

"Nihilist?"

Jakes chuckled. "When you've been in this Section for a while, you'll be familiar with every screwball outfit man has ever dreamed up. The Nihilists were a European group, mostly Russian, back in the Nineteenth Century. They believed that by bumping off a few Grand Dukes and a Czar or so they could force the ruling class to grant reforms. Sometimes they were pretty ingenious. Blew up trains, that sort of thing."

"Look here," Ronny said, "what motivates this Paine fellow? What's he get out of all this trouble he stirs up?"

"Search me. Nobody seems to know. Some think he's a mental case. For one thing, he's not consistent."

"How do you mean?"

"Well, he'll go to one planet and break his back trying to overthrow, say, feudalism. Then, possibly after being suc-

19

cessful, he goes to another planet and devotes his energies to establishing the same socio-economic system."

Ronny assimilated that. "You're one of those who believes he exists?"

"Oh, he exists, all right, all right," Sid Jakes said happily. "Matter of fact, I almost ran into him a few years ago."

Ronny leaned forward. "I guess I ought to know about it. The more information I have, the better."

"Sure, sure," Jakes said. "This deal of mine was on one of the Aldebaran planets. A bunch of nature boys had settled there."

"Nature boys?"

"Yeah. Back to nature. The trouble with the human race is that it's got too far away from nature. So a whole flock of them landed on this planet. They call it Mother, of all things. They landed and set up a primitive society. Absolute stone age. No metals. Lived by the chase and by picking berries, wild fruit, that sort of thing. Not even any agriculture. Wore skins. Bows and arrows were the nearest thing they allowed themselves in the way of mechanical devices."

"Good grief," Ronny said.

"It was a laugh," Jakes told him. "I was assigned there as Section G representative with the UP organization. Picture it. We had to wear skins for clothes. We had to confine ourselves to two or three long houses. Something like the American Iroquois lived in before Columbus. Their society on Mother was based on primitive communism. The clan, the phratry, the tribe. Their religion was mostly a matter of knocking into everybody's head that any progress was taboo. Oh, it was great."

"Well, were they happy?"

"What's happiness? I suppose they were as happy as anybody ever averages. Frankly, I didn't mind the assignment. Lots of fishing, lots of hunting."

Ronny said, "Well, where does Tommy Paine come in?"

"He snuck up on us. Started way back in the boondocks away from any of the larger primitive settlements. Went around putting himself over as a holy man. Cured people of various things from gangrene to eye diseases. Given antibiotics and such, you can imagine how successful he was."

"Well, what harm did he do?"

"I didn't say he did any harm. But in that manner he made himself awfully popular. Then he'd pull some trick like showing them how to smelt iron, and distribute some corn and wheat seed around and plant the idea of agriculture. The local witch doctors would try to give him a hard time, but the people figured he was a holy man."

"Well, what happened finally?" Ronny wasn't following too well.

"Communications being what they were, before he'd been discovered by the central organization—they had a kind of Council of Tribes which met once a year—he'd planted so many ideas that they couldn't be stopped. The young people'd never go back to flint knives, once introduced to iron. We went looking for friend Tommy Paine, but he got wind of it and took off. We even found where he'd hidden his little space cruiser. Oh, it was Paine, all right, all right."

"But what harm did he do? I don't understand," Ronny scowled.

"He threw everything on its ear. Last I heard, the planet had broken up into three main camps. They were whaling away at each other like the Assyrians and Egyptians. Iron weapons, chariots, domesticated horses. Agriculture was sweeping the planet. Population was exploding. Men were making slaves out of each other, to put them to work. Oh, it was a mess from the viewpoint of the original nature boys."

A red light flickered on his desk and Sid Jakes opened a delivery drawer and dipped his hand into it. It emerged with a flat wallet. He tossed it to Ronny Bronston.

"Here you are. Your badge."

Ronny opened the wallet and examined it. He'd never seen one before, but for that matter he'd never heard of Section G before that morning. It was a simple enough bronze badge. It said merely, *Ronald Bronston, Section G, Bureau of Investigation, United Planets.*

Sid Jakes explained. "You'll get cooperation with that

21

through the Justice Department anywhere you go. We'll brief you further on procedure during indoctrination. You in turn, of course, are to coöperate with any other agent of Section G. You're under orders of anyone with"—his hand snaked into a pocket and emerged with a wallet similar to Ronny's—"a silver badge, carried by a First Grade Agent, or a gold one of Supervisor rank."

Ronny noted that his badge wasn't really bronze. It had a certain sheen, a brightness.

Jake said, "Here, look at this." He tossed his own badge to the new man. Ronny looked down at it in surprise. The gold had gone dull.

Jakes laughed. "Now give me yours."

Ronny got up and walked over to him and handed it over. As soon as the other man's hand touched it, the bronze lost its sheen.

Jakes handed it back. "See, it's tuned to you alone," he said. "And mine is tuned to my code. Nobody can swipe a Section G badge and impersonate an agent. If anybody ever shows you a badge that doesn't have its sheen, you know he's a fake. Neat trick, eh?"

"Very neat," Ronny admitted. He returned the other's gold badge. "Look, to get back to this Tommy Paine."

But the red light flickered again and Jakes brought forth from the delivery drawer a hand gun complete with shoulder harness. "Nasty weapon," he said. "But we'd better go on down to the armory and show you its workings."

He stood up. "Oh, yes, don't let me forget to give you a communicator. A real gizmo. About as big as a woman's vanity case. Puts you in immediate contact with the nearest Section G office, no matter how near or far away it is. Or, if you wish, in contact with our offices here in the Octagon. Very neat trick."

He led Ronny Bronston from his office and down the corridors beyond to an elevator. He said happily, "This is a crazy outfit, this Section G. You'll probably love it. Everybody does."

III

RONNY LEARNED to love Section G—in moderation.

He was initially taken aback by the existence of the organization at all. He'd known, of course, of the Department of Justice and even of the Bureau of Investigation, but Section G was hush-hush and not even United Planets publications ever mentioned it.

The problems involved in remaining hush-hush weren't as great as all that. The very magnitude of the UP, which involved more than two thousand member planets, allowed for departments and bureaus hidden away in the endless stretches of red tape.

In fact, although Ronny Bronston had spent the better part of his life thus far in studying for a place in the organization, and then working in the Population Statistics Department for some years, he was only now beginning to get the overall picture of the workings of the mushrooming, chaotic United Planets organization.

It was Earth's largest industry by far. In fact, for all practical purposes it was her only major industry. Tourism, yes, but even that, in a way, was related to the United Planets organization. Millions of visitors whose ancestors had once emigrated from the mother planet streamed back in racial nostalgia. Streamed back to see the continents and oceans, the Arctic and the Antarctic, the Amazon River and Mount Everest, the Sahara and New York City, the ruins of Rome and Athens, the Vatican, the Louvre and the Hermitage.

But the populace of Earth, in its hundreds of millions, were largely citizens of United Planets and worked in the organization and with its auxiliaries such as the Space Forces.

Section G? To his surprise, Ronny found that Ross Metaxa's small section of the Bureau of Investigation seemed almost as great a secret within the Bureau as it was to the man in the street. At one period, Ronny wondered if it were

23

possible that this was a department which had been lost in the wilderness of boondoggling that goes on in any great bureaucracy. Had Section G been set up a century or so ago and then forgotten by those who had originally thought there was a need for it? In the same way that it is usually more difficult to get a statute off the lawbooks than it was originally to pass it, eliminating an office, with its employees, can prove more difficult than originally establishing it.

But that wasn't it. In spite of the informality, the unconventional brashness of its personnel on all levels, and the seeming chaos in which its tasks were done, Section G was no make-work project set up to provide juicy jobs for the relatives of high ranking officials. To the contrary, it didn't take long in the Section before anybody with open eyes could see that Ross Metaxa was privy to the decisions made by the upper echelons of UP.

Ronny Bronston came to the conclusion that the appointment he'd received was putting him in a higher bracket of the UP hierarchy than he'd at first imagined.

His indoctrination course was a strain such as he'd never known in school years. Ross Metaxa was evidently of the opinion that a man could assimilate concentrated information at a rate several times faster than any professional educator ever dreamed possible. No threats were made, but Ronny realized that he could be dropped even more quickly than he'd seemed to have been taken on. There were no classes, to either push or retard the rate of study. He worked with a series of tutors, and pushed himself. The tutors were almost invariably Section G agents, temporarily in Greater Washington between assignments, or for briefing on this phase or that of their work.

Even as he studied, Ronny Bronston kept in mind the eventual assignment at which he was to prove himself. He made a point of inquiring of each agent he met about Tommy Paine.

The name was known to all, but no two reacted in the same manner. Several of them even brushed the whole matter aside as pure legend. *Nobody* could accomplish all the trouble that Tommy Paine had supposedly stirred up.

To one of these, Ronny said plaintively, "Look, the Old Man believes in him, Sid Jakes believes in him. My final appointment depends on arresting him. How can I ever secure this job, if I'm chasing a myth?"

The other shrugged. "Don't ask me. I've got my own problems. O.K., now, let's run over this question of Napoleonic law. There are at least two hundred planets that base their legal system on it."

But the majority of his fellow employees in Section G had strong enough opinions on the interplanetary firebrand. Three or four even claimed to have seen him fleetingly, although no two descriptions jibed. That, of course, could be explained. The man could resort to plastic surgery and other disguises.

Theories there were in plenty, some of them going back long years, and some of them pure fable.

"Look," Ronny said in disgust one day after a particularly unbelievable siege with two agents recently returned from a trouble spot in a planetary system that involved three aggressive worlds which revolved about the same sun. "Look, it's impossible for one man to accomplish all this. He's blamed for half the *coups d'états*, revolts and upheavals that have taken place for the past quarter century. It's obvious nonsense. Why, a revolutionist usually spends the greater part of his life toppling a government. Then, once it toppled, he spends the rest of his life trying to set up a new government —and he's usually unsuccessful."

One of the others was shaking his head negatively. "You don't understand this Tommy Paine's system, Bronston."

The other agent, a Nigerian, grinned widely. "You sure don't. I've been on planets where he'd operated."

Ronny leaned forward. The three of them were having a beer in a part of the city once called Baltimore. "You have?" he said. "Tell me about it, eh? The more background I get on this guy, the better."

"Sure. And this'll give you an idea of how he operates,

how he can get so much trouble done. Well, I was on this
planet Goshen, understand? It had kind of a strange history.
A bunch of colonists went out there, oh, four or five centuries
ago. Pretty healthy expedition, as such outfits go. Bright
young people, lots of equipment, lots of know-how and books.
Well, through sheer bad luck everything went wrong from
the beginning. Everything. Before they got set up at all they
had an explosion that killed off all their communications tech-
nicians. They lost contact with the outside. O.K. Within a
couple of centuries they'd gotten into a state of chattel slavery. Pretty well organized, but static. Kind of an Athenian
Democracy on top, a hierarchy, but nineteen people out of
twenty were slaves, and I mean *real* slaves, like animals. They
were at this stage when a scout ship from the UP Space
Forces discovered them and, of course, they joined up."

"Where does Tommy Paine come in?" Ronny said. He
signaled to a waiter for more beer.

"He comes in a few years later. I was the Section G agent
on Goshen, understand? No planet was keener about Articles
One and Two of the UP Charter. The hierarchy understood
well enough that if their people ever came to know about
more advanced socio-economic systems it'd be the end of
Goshen's Golden Age. So they allowed practically no intercourse. No contact whatsoever between UP personnel and
anyone outside the upper class, understand? All right. That's
where Tommy Paine came in. It couldn't have taken him
more than a couple of months at most."

Ronny Bronston was fascinated. "What'd he do?"

"He introduced the steam engine, and then left."

Ronny was looking at him blankly. "Steam engine?"

"That and the fly shuttle and the spinning jenny," the
Nigerian said. "That Goshen hierarchy never knew what hit
them."

Ronny was still blank. The waiter came up with the steins
of beer, and Ronny took one and drained half of it without
taking his eyes from the storyteller.

The other agent took it up. "Don't you see? Their system
was based on chattel slavery, hand labor. Given machinery

26

and it collapses. Chattel slavery isn't practical in a mechan-
ized society. Too expensive a labor force, for one thing. Besides, you need an educated man and one with some initia-
tive—qualities that few slaves possess—to run an industrial
society."

Ronny finished his beer. "Smart cooky, isn't he?"

"He's smart, all right. But I've got a still better example
of his fouling up a whole planetary socio-economic system
in a matter of weeks. A friend of mine was working on a
planet with a highly-developed feudalism. Barons, lords,
dukes, counts and no-accounts, all stashed safely away
in castles and fortresses up on the top of hills. The serfs
down below did all the work in the fields, provided servants,
artisans and foot soldiers for the continual fighting that the
aristocracy carried on. Very similar to Europe back in the
Dark Ages."

"So?" Ronny said. "I'd think that'd be a deal that would
take centuries to change."

The Section G agent laughed. "Tommy Paine stayed just
long enough to introduce gunpowder. That was the end of
those impregnable castles up on the hills."

"What gets me," Ronny said slowly, "is his motivation."

The other two both grunted agreement to that.

IV

TOWARD THE END of his indoctrination studies, Ronny appeared one morning at the Octagon Section G offices and
before Irene Kasansky. Watching her fingers fly, listening to
her voice rapping and snapping, O.K.ing and rejecting, he
came to the conclusion that automation could go just so far in
office work and then you were thrown back on the hands of
the efficient secretary. Irene was a one-woman office staff.

She looked up at him. "Hello, Ronny. Thought you'd be
off on your assignment by now. Got any clues on Tommy
Paine?"

27

"No," he said. "That's why I'm here. I wanted to see the commissioner."

"About what?" She flicked a switch. When a light flickered on one of her order-boxes, she said into it, "No," emphatically, and turned back to him.

"He said he wanted to see me again before I took off."

She fiddled some more, finally said, "All right, Ronny. Tell him he's got time for five minutes with you."

"Five minutes!"

. "Then he's got an appointment with the Commissioner of Interplanetary Culture," she said. "You'd better hurry along."

Ronny Bronston retraced the route of his first visit here. How long ago? It already seemed ages since his probationary appointment. Your life changed fast when you were in Section G.

Ross Metaxa's brown bottle, or its twin, was sitting on his desk and he was staring at it glumly. He looked up and scowled.

"Ronald Bronston," Ronny said. "Irene Kasansky told me to say I could have five minutes with you, and then you have an appointment with the Commissioner of Interplanetary Culture."

"I remember you," Metaxa said. "Have a drink. Interplanetary Culture, ha! The Xanadu Folk Dance Troupe. They dance nude. They've been touring the whole UP. Roaring success everywhere, obviously. Now they're assigned to Virtue, a planet settled by a bunch of Fundamentalists. They want the troupe to wear Mother Hubbards. The Xanadu outfit is in a tizzy. They've been insulted. They claim they're the most modest members of UP, that nudity has nothing to do with modesty. The government of Virtue says that's fine but they wear Mother Hubbards or they don't dance. Xanadu says it'll withdraw from United Planets."

Ronny Bronston said painfully, "Why not let them?"

Ross Metaxa poured himself a Denebian tequila, offered his subordinate a drink again with a motion of the bottle. Ronny shook his head.

Metaxa said, "If we didn't take steps to soothe these

28

things over, there wouldn't be any United Planets. In any given century every member in the organization threatens to resign at least once. Even Earth. And then what'd happen? You'd have interplanetary war before you knew it. What'd you want, Ronny?"

"I'm about set to take up my search for this Tommy Paine."

"Ah, yes, Tommy Paine. If you catch him, there are a dozen planets where he'd be eligible for the death sentence."

Ronny cleared his throat. "There must be. What I wanted was the file on him, sir."

"File?"

"Yes, sir. I've got to the point where I want to cram up on everything we have on him. So far, all I've got is verbal information from individual agents and from Supervisor Jakes."

"Don't be silly, Ronny. There isn't any file on Tommy Paine."

Ronny stared at him.

Ross Metaxa said impatiently, "The very knowledge of the existence of the man is top secret. Isn't that obvious? Suppose some reporter got the story and printed it. If our member planets knew there was such a man and that we haven't been able to scotch him, why, they'd drop out of UP so fast the computers couldn't keep up with it. There's not one planet in ten that feels secure enough to lay itself open to subversion. Why, some of our planets are so far down the ladder of social evolution they live under primitive tribal society; their leaders, their wise men and witch-doctors, whatever you call them, are scared someone will come along and establish chattel slavery. Those planets that have a system based on slavery are scared to death of developing feudalism, and those that have feudalism are afraid of *creeping capitalism*. Those with an anarchistic basis—and we have several—are afraid of being subverted to statism, and those who have a highly developed government are afraid of anarchism. The socio-economic systems based on private ownership of property hate the very idea of socialism

29

or communism, and vice versa, and those planets with state capitalism hate them both."

He glared at Ronny. "What do you think the purpose of this Section is, Bronston? Our job is to keep our member planets from being afraid of each other. If they found that Tommy Paine and his group, if he's got a group, were buzzing through the system subverting everything they could foul up, they'd drop out of UP and set up quarantines that a space mite couldn't get through. No sir, there is no file on Tommy Paine and there never will be. And if any news of him spreads to the outside, this Section will emphatically deny he exists. I hope that's clear."

"Well, yes, sir," Ronny said. The commissioner had been all but roaring toward the end.

The order box clicked on Ross Metaxa's desk and he said loudly, "What?"

"Don't yell at me," Irene snapped back. "Ronny's five minutes are up. You've got an appointment. I'm getting tired of this job. It's a madhouse. I'm going to quit and get a job with Interplanetary Finance."

"Oh, yeah," Ross snarled. "That's what you think. I've taken measures. Top security. I've warned off every Commissioner in UP. You can't get away from me until you reach retirement age. Although I don't know why I care. I hate nasty tempered women."

"Huh!" she snorted and clicked off.

"There's a woman for you," Ross Metaxa growled at Ronny. "It's too bad she's indispensable. I'd love to fire her. Look, you go in and see Sid Jakes. Seems to me he said something about Tommy Paine this morning. Maybe it's a lead." He came to his feet. "So long and good luck, Ronny. I feel optimistic about you. I think you'll get this Paine troublemaker."

Which was more than Ronny Bronston thought.

Sid Jakes already had a visitor in his office, which didn't prevent him from yelling, "It's open," when Ronny Bronston knocked.

He bounced from his chair, came around the desk and shook hands enthusiastically. "Ronny!" he said, his tone implying they were favorite brothers for long years parted. "You're just in time."

Ronny took in the office's other occupant appreciatively. She was a small girl, almost tiny. He estimated her to be at least half Chinese, or maybe Indo-Chinese, the rest probably European or North American. She evidently favored her Asiatic blood—her dress was traditional Chinese, slit almost to the thigh Shanghai style.

Sid Jakes said, "Tog Lee Chang Chu . . . Ronny Bronston. You'll be working together. Bloodhounding old Tommy Paine. A neat trick if you can pull it off. Well, are you all set to go?"

Ronny mumbled something to the girl in the way of amenity, then looked back at the supervisor. "Working together?" he said.

"That's right. Lucky you, eh?"

Tog Lee Chang Chu said demurely, "Possibly Mr. Bronston objects to having a female assistant."

Sid Jakes snorted, and hurried around his desk to resume his seat. "Does he look crazy? Who'd object to having you around day in and day out? Call him Ronny. Might as well get used to it. The two of you'll be closer than man and wife."

"Assistant?" Ronny said, bewildered. "What do I need an assistant for?" He turned his eyes to the girl. "No reflection on you, Miss . . . ah, Tog."

Sid Jakes laughed easily. "Section G operatives always work in pairs, Ronny. Especially new agents. The advantages will come home to you as you go along. Look on Tog Lee Chang Chu as a secretary, a gal Friday. This isn't her first assignment, of course. You'll find her invaluable."

The supervisor plucked a card from an order box. "Now, here's the dope. Can you leave within four hours? There's a UP Space Force cruiser going to Merlini; they can drop you off at New Delos. Fastest way you could possibly get there. The cruiser takes off from Neuve Alburquerque in, let's see, three hours and forty-five minutes."

"New Delos?" Ronny said, taking his eyes from the girl and trying to catch up with the grasshopper-like conversation of his superior.

"New Delos it is," Jakes said happily. "With luck, you might catch him before he can get off the planet." He chuckled at the other's expression. "Look alive, Ronny! The quarry is flushed and on the run. Tommy Paine's just assassinated the Immortal God-King of New Delos. A neat trick, eh?"

V

THE FOLLOWING HOURS were chaotic. There was no indication of how long a period he'd be gone. For all he knew, it might be years. For that matter, he might never return to Earth. This Ronny Bronston had realized before he'd ever applied for an interplanetary appointment. Mankind was exploding through this spiral arm of the galaxy. There was a racial enthusiasm about it all. Man's destiny lay out in the stars; only a laggard stayed home of his own accord. It was the ambition of every youth to join the snowballing avalanche of man into the neighboring stars.

It took absolute severity by Earth authorities to prevent the depopulation of the planet. But someone had to stay to administer the ever more complicated racial destiny. Earth became a clearing house for a thousand cultures, attempting, with only moderate success, to coördinate her widely spreading children. She couldn't afford to let her best seed depart. Few were allowed to emigrate from Earth anymore. New colonies drew their immigrants from older ones.

Lucky was the Earthling able to find service in interplanetary affairs, in any of the thousands of tasks that involved journey between member planets of UP. Possibly one hundredth of the population at one time or another, and for varying lengths of time, managed it.

Ronny Bronston was lucky and knew it. The thing now was to pull off this assignment and cinch the appointment for good.

He packed in a swirl of confusion. He phoned a relative who lived in the part of town once known as Richmond, explained the situation and asked that the other store his things and dispose of the apartment he'd been occupying.

Luckily, the roof of his apartment building was a coptercab pickup point and he was able to hustle over to the shuttleport in a matter of a few minutes.

He banged into the reservations office, hurried up to one of the windows and said into the screen, "I've got to get to Neuve Alburquerque immediately."

The expressionless voice said, "The next rocket leaves at sixteen hours."

"Sixteen hours! I've got to be at the spaceport by that time!"

The voice said dispassionately, "We are sorry."

The bottom fell out of everything. Ronny said, desperately, "Look, if I miss my ship in Neuve Alburquerque, what is the next spaceliner leaving from there for New Delos?"

"A moment, citizen." There was an agonized wait, and then the voice said, "There is a liner leaving for New Delos on the 14th of next month. It arrives in New Delos on the 31st, Basic Earth calendar."

The 31st! Tommy Paine could be halfway across the galaxy by that time.

A gentle voice next to him said, "Could I help, Ronny?"

He looked around at her. "Evidently, nobody can," he said disgustedly. "There's no way of getting to Neuve Albuquerque in time to get that cruiser to New Delos."

Tog Lee Chang Chu fished in her bag and came up with a wallet similar to the one in which Ronny carried his Section G badge. She held it up to the screen. "Bureau of Investigation, Section G," she said calmly. "It will be necessary that Agent Bronston and I be in Neuve Albuquerque within the hour."

The metallic voice said, "Of course. Proceed to your

right and through Corridor K to Exit Four. Your rocket will be there. Identify yourself to Lieutenant Economou, who will be at the desk at Exit Four."

Tog turned to Ronny Bronston. "Shall we go?" she said demurely.

He cleared his throat, feeling foolish. "Thanks, Tog," he said.

"Not at all, Ronny. Why, this is my job."

Was there the faintest touch of sarcasm in her voice? It hadn't been more than a couple of hours ago that he had been hinting rather heavily to Sid Jakes that he needed no assistance.

She even knew the layout of the West Greater Washington shuttleport. Her small body swiveled through the hurrying passengers, her small feet a-twinkle, as she led him to and down Corridor K and then to the desk at Exit Four.

Ronny anticipated her here. He flashed his own badge at the chairborne Space Forces lieutenant there.

"Lieutenant Economou?" he said. "Ronald Bronston, of the Bureau of Investigation, Section G. We've got to get to Neuve Alburquerque soonest."

The lieutenant, only mildly impressed, said, "We can have you in the air in ten minutes, citizen. Just a moment and I'll guide you myself."

In the rocket, Ronny had time to appraise her at greater length. She was a delicately pretty thing, although her expression was inclined to the over-serious. There was only a touch of the Mongolian fold at the corner of her eyes. On her it looked unusually good. Her complexion was that which only the blend of Chinese and Caucasian can give. Her figure, thanks to her European blood, was fuller than Eastern Asia usually boasts; tiny, but full.

Let's admit it, he decided. *My assistant is the cutest trick this side of a Tri-D movie queen, and we're going to be thrown in the closest of juxtaposition for an indefinite time. This comes under the head of work?*

He said, "Look here, Tog, you were with Sid Jakes longer than I was. What's the full story?"

She folded her slim hands in her lap, looking like a schoolgirl about to recite. "Do you know anything about the socio-economic system on New Delos?"

"Well, no," he admitted.

She said severely, "I'd think that they would have given you more background before an assignment of this type."

Ronny said impatiently, "In the past three months I've been filled in on the economic systems, the religious beliefs, the political forms, of a thousand planets. I just happened to miss New Delos."

Her mouth expressed disapproval by tucking down on the sides, which was all very attractive but also irritating. She said, "There are two thousand, four hundred and thirty-six member planets in the UP—I'd think an agent of Section G would be up on the basic situation on each."

He had her there. He said snidely, "Hate to contradict you, Tog, but the number is two thousand, four hundred and thirty-four."

"Then," she nodded agreeably, "membership has changed since this morning when Menalaus and Aldeberan Three were admitted. Have two planets dropped out?"

"Look," he said, "let's stop bickering. What's the word on New Delos?"

"Did you ever read Frazer's *Golden Bough?*" she asked.

"No."

"You should. At any rate, New Delos is a theocracy. A priesthood elite rules it. A God-King, who is immortal, holds absolute authority. The strongest of superstition, plus an efficient inquisition, keeps the people under control."

"Sounds terrible," Ronny growled.

"Why? Possibly the government is extremely efficient and under it the planet progressing at a rate in advance of UP averages."

He stared at her in surprise.

She said, "Would you rather be ruled by the personal

arbitrary whims of supremely wise men, or by laws formulated by a mob?"

It stopped him momentarily. In all his adult years, he couldn't remember ever meeting an intelligent, educated person who had been opposed to the democratic theory.

"Wait a minute, now," he said. "Who decides that they're supremely wise men who are doing this arbitrary ruling? Let any group come to power, by whatever means, and they'll soon tell you they're an elite. But let's get back to New Delos—from what you've said so far, the people are held in a condition of slavery."

"What's wrong with slavery?" Tog said mildly.

He all but glared at her. "Are you kidding?"

"I seldom jest," Tog said primly. "Under the proper conditions, slavery can be the most suitable system for a people."

"Under *what* conditions?"

"Have you forgotten your Earth history to the point where Egypt, Greece and Rome mean nothing to you? Man made some of his outstanding progress under slavery. And do you contend that man's lot is necessarily miserable given slavery? As far back as Aesop we know of slaves who have reached the heights in their society. Slaves sometimes could and did become the virtual rulers in ancient countries." She shrugged prettily. "The prejudices which you hold today, on Earth, do not necessarily apply to all time, nor to all places."

He said impatiently, "Look, Tog, we can go into this further later. Let's get back to New Delos. What happened?"

Tog said, "The very foundation of their theocracy is the belief on the part of the populace that the God-King is immortal. No man conspires against his Diety. Supervisor Jakes informed me that it is understood by UP Intelligence that about once every twenty years the priesthood secretly puts in a new God-King. Plastic surgery would guarantee facial resemblance, and, of course, the rank and file citizen would probably never be allowed close enough to discover that their God-King seemed different every couple of decades. At any rate, it's been working for some time."

"And there's been no revolt against this religious aristocracy?"

She shook her head. "Evidently not. It takes a brave man to revolt against both his king and his God at the same time."

"But what happened now?" Ronny pursued.

"Evidently, right in the midst of a particularly important religious ceremony, with practically the whole planet watching on TV, the God-King was killed with a bomb. No doubt about it, definitely killed. There are going to be a lot of people on New Delos wondering how it can be that an immortal God-King can die."

"And Sid thinks it's Tommy Paine's work?"

She shifted dainty shoulders in a shrug. "It's the sort of thing he does. I suppose we'll learn when we get there."

VI

EVEN ON THE fast Space Forces cruiser, the trip was going to take a week, and there was precious little Ronny Bronston could do until arrival. He spent most of his time reading up on New Delos and the several other planets in the UP organization which had fairly similar regimes. More than a few theocracies had come and gone during the history of man's development into the stars.

He also spent considerable time playing Battle Chess or talking with Tog and with the ship's officers.

These latter were a dedicated group, high in morale and enthusiastic about their work, which evidently involved the combined duties of a Navy, a Coast Guard, and a Coast and Geodetic Survey system, if we use the ocean going services of an earlier age for analogy.

They all had the dream. The enthusiasm of men participating in a race's expansion to glory. There was the feeling, even stronger here in space than back on Earth, that man's destiny was being fulfilled, that humanity had finally emerged from its infancy, that the fledgling had finally found its wings and got off the ground.

PLANETARY AGENT X

After one of his studying binges, Ronny Bronston spent an hour or so once with the captain of the craft, while that officer stood an easy watch on the ship's bridge. There was little enough to do in space, practically nothing, but there was always an officer on watch.

They leaned back in the acceleration chairs before the ship's controls and Ronny listened to the other's space lore. Stories of far planets, as yet untouched. Stories of planets that had seemingly been suitable for colonization, but had proved disastrous for man, for this reason or that.

Ronny said, "And never in all this time have we run into a life form that has proved intelligent?"

Captain Woiski said, "No. Not that I know of. There was an animal on Shangri-La of about the mental level of the chimpanzee. So far as I know, that's the nearest to it."

"Shangri-La?" Ronny said. "That's a new one."

There was an affectionate gleam in the captain's eye. "Yes," he said. "If and when I retire, I think that'd be the planet of my choice. If I could get permission to leave Earth, of course."

Ronny scowled in attempted memory. "Now that you mention it, I think I did see it listed the other day among planets with a theocratic government."

The captain grunted protest. "If you're comparing it to this New Delos you're going to, you're wrong. There can be theocracy and theocracy, I suppose. Actually, I imagine Shangri-La has the most, well *gentle* government in the system."

Ronny was interested. His recent studies hadn't led him to much respect for a priesthood in political power. "What's the particular feature that's seemed to have gained your regard?"

"Moderation," Woiski chuckled. "They carry it almost to the point of immoderation. But not quite. Briefly, it works something like this. They have a limited number of monks— I suppose you'd call them that—who spend their time at whatever moves them. At the arts, at scientific research, at religious contemplation—any religion will do—as students of

anything and everything, and at the governing of Shangri-La.
They make a point of enjoying the luxuries in moderation
and aren't a severe drain on the rank and file citizens of the
planet."

Ronny said, "I have a growing distrust of hierarchies.
Who decides who is to become a monk and who remain a
member of the rank and file?"

The captain said, "A series of the best tests they can devise to determine a person's intelligence and aptitudes.
From earliest youth, the whole populace is checked and re-
checked. At the age of thirty, when it is considered that a
person has become an adult and has finished his basic
education, a limited number are offered monkhood. Not all
want it."

Ronny thought about it. "Why not? What are the short-
comings?"

The captain shrugged. "Responsibility, I suppose."

"The monks aren't allowed sex, booze, that sort of thing,
I imagine."

"Good heavens, why not? In moderation, of course."

"And they live on a higher scale?"

"No, no, not at all. Don't misunderstand. The planet is
a prosperous one. Exceedingly prosperous. There is everything needed for comfortable existence for everyone. Shangri-
La is one planet where the pursuit of happiness is pursuable
by all." Captain Woiski chuckled again.

Ronny said, "It sounds good enough, although I'm leary
of benevolent dictatorships. The trouble with them is that it's
up to the dictators to decide what's benevolent. And almost
always, nepotism rears its head, favoritism of one sort or another. How long will it be before one of your moderate monks
decides he'll moderately tinker with the tests, or whatever,
just to be sure his favorite nephew makes the grade? A high
I.Q. is no guarantee of integrity."

The captain didn't disagree. "That's always possible, I
suppose. One guard against it, in this case, is the matter of
motive. The *privilege* of being a monk isn't as great as all
that. Materially, you aren't particularly better off than any

39

one else. You have more leisure, that's true, but actually most of them are so caught up in their studies or research that they put in more hours of endeavor than does the farmer or industrial worker on Shangri-La."

"Well," Ronny said, "let's just hope that Tommy Paine never hears of this place."

"Who?" the captain said.

Ronny Bronston reversed his engines. "Oh, nobody important. A guy I know of."

Captain Woiski scowled. "Seems to me I've heard the name."

At first Ronny leaned forward with quick interest. Perhaps the cruiser's skipper had a lead. But, no, he sank back into his chair. That name was strictly a Section G pseudonym. No one used it outside the department, and he'd already said too much by using the term at all.

Ronny said idly, "Probably two different people. I think I'll go on back and see how Tog is doing."

Tog was at her communicator when he entered the tiny ship's lounge. Ronny could see, in the brilliant little screen of the compact device, the grinning face of Sid Jakes. Tog looked up at Ronny and smiled, then clicked the device off.

"What's new?" Ronny said.

She moved graceful shoulders. "I just called Supervisor Jakes. Evidently there's complete confusion on New Delos. Mobs are storming the temples. In the capital the priests tried to present a new God-King and he was laughed out of town."

Ronny snorted cynically. "Sounds good to me. The more I read about New Delos and its God-King and his priesthood, the more I think the best thing that ever happened to the planet was this showing them up."

Tog looked at him, the sides of her mouth tucking down as usual when she was going to contradict something he said. "It sounds bad to me," she said. "Tommy Paine's work is done. He'll be off to some other place and we won't get there in time to snare him."

Ronny considered that. It was probably true. "I wonder,"

PLANETARY AGENT X

he said slowly, "if it's possible for us to get a list of all ships that have blasted off since the assassination, all ships and their destination from New Delos."

The idea grew in him. "Look! It's possible that a dictatorial government such as theirs would immediately quarantine every spaceport on the planet."

Tog said, "There's only one spaceport on New Delos. The priesthood didn't encourage trade or even communication with the outside. Didn't want its people contaminated."

"Good God!" Ronny blurted. "It's possible that Tommy Paine's on that planet and can't get off. Look, Tog, see if you can raise the Section G representative on New Delos and—"

Tog said demurely, "I already have taken that step, Ronny, knowing that you'd want me to. Agent Mouley Hassan has promised to get the name and destination of every passenger that leaves New Delos."

Ronny sat down at a table and dialed himself a mug of stout. "Drink?" he said to Tog. "Possibly we've got something to celebrate."

She shook her head disapprovingly. "I don't use depressants."

There was nothing more to be discussed about New Delos; they simply would have to wait until their arrival. Ronny switched subjects. "Ever hear of the planet Shangri-La?" he asked her. He took a sip of his brew.

"Of course," she said. "A rather small planet, Earth type within four degrees. Noted for its near perfect climate and its scenic beauty."

"Captain was talking about it," Ronny said. "Sounds like a regular paradise."

Tog made a negative sound.

"Well, what's wrong with Shangri-La?" Ronny said impatiently.

"Static," she said briefly.

He looked at her. "It sounds to me as though it's developed a near perfect socio-economic system. What do you mean, static?"

41

"No push, no drive," Tog said definitely. "Everyone—what is the old term?—everyone has it made. The place is stagnating. I wouldn't be surprised to see Tommy Paine show up there sooner or later."

Ronny said, "Look, since we've known each other, have I ever said anything you agree with?"

Tog raised her delicate eyebrows. "Why, Ronny. You know perfectly well we both agreed that the eggs for breakfast were quite inedibble."

Ronny came to his feet again. Considering her size, she certainly was an irritating baggage. "I think I'll go to my room and see if I can get any inspirations on tracking down our quarry."

"Good night, Ronny," she said demurely.

VII

THEY RAN INTO a minor difficulty upon arrival at New Delos. The captain called both Ronny Bronston and Tog Lee Chang Chu to the bridge.

He nodded in the direction of the communications screen. A bald headed, robed character, obviously a priest, scowled at them.

Captain Woiski said, "The Sub-Bishop informs me that the provisional government has ruled that any spacecraft landing on New Delos cannot take off again without permission and that every individual who lands, even United Planets personnel, will need an exit visa before being allowed to depart."

Ronny said, "Then you can't land?"

The captain said reasonably, "My destination is Merlini. I've gone out of my way slightly to drop you off here. But I can't afford to take the chance of having my ship tied up for what might be an indefinite period. Evidently there's considerable civil disorder down there."

From the screen the priest snapped, "That is an inaccurate manner of describing the situation."

"Sorry," the captain said dryly.

Ronny Bronston said desperately, "But, captain, Miss Tog and I simply have to land." He reached for his badge. "High priority, Bureau of Investigations."

The captain shrugged his hefty shoulders. "Sorry, I have no instructions that allow me to risk tying up my ship. Here's a possibility. Can you pilot a landing craft? I could spare you one—then you and your assistant would be the only ones involved. You could turn it over to whatever Space Forces base we have here."

Ronny said miserably, "No, I'm not a space pilot."

"I am," Tog said softly. "The idea sounds excellent."

"We shall expect you," the Sub-Bishop said. The screen went blank.

Tog Lee Chang Chu piloted a landing craft with the same verve that she seemed to be able to handle any other responsibility. As he sat in the seat next to her, Ronny Bronston took in her practiced flicking of the controls from the side of his eyes. He wondered vaguely at the efficiency of such Section G officials as Metaxa and Jakes that they would assign an unknown quality such as himself to a task as important as running down Tommy Paine, and then as an assistant provide him with an experienced operative such as Tog. The bureaucratic mind could be a dilly, he decided. Was the fact that she was a rather delicately constructed girl a factor? He felt the weight of the Model-H gun nestled under his left armpit. Perhaps in the clutch Section G preferred men as agents.

They swooped into a landing that brought them as close to the control tower as was practical. In a matter of moments there was a guard of twenty or more sloppily uniformed men about their small craft.

Tog made a *moue*. "Welcoming committee," she said.

They climbed out the circular port, and Ronny flashed his United Planets Bureau of Investigation badge at the youngish looking soldier who seemed in command. He was indecisive.

"United Planets?" he said. "All I know is I'm supposed to arrest anybody landing."

Ronny snapped, "We're to be taken immediately to United Planets headquarters."

"Well, I don't know about that. I don't take orders from foreigners."

One of his men was nervously fingering the trigger of his submachine gun.

Ronny's mouth went dry. He had the feeling of being high, high on a rock face, inadequately belayed from above.

Tog said smoothly, "But major, I'm sure whoever issued your orders had no expectation of a special delegation from the United Planets coming to congratulate your new authorities on their success. Of course, it's unknown to arrest a delegation from United Planets."

"It is?" he frowned at her. "I mean, you are?"

"Yes," Tog said sweetly.

Ronny took the hint. "Where can we find a vehicle, major, to get us the capital and to United Planets headquarters? Evidently we arrived before we were expected. There should have been a big welcoming committee here."

"Oh," the obviously recently promoted lad said hesitantly. "Well, I suppose we can make arrangements. This way, please." He grinned at Tog as they walked toward the administration building. "Do all girls dress like you on Earth?"

"Well, no," she said demurely.

"That's too bad," he said gallantly.

"Why, major!" Tog said, keeping her eyes on the tarmac.

At the administration building there was little of order, but eventually they managed to arrange for their transportation. Luckily, they were supplied with a chauffeur driven heliocar.

Luckily, because without the chauffeur to help them run the gauntlet they would have been held up by parades, demonstrations and monstrous street meetings a dozen times before they ever reached their destination. Twice Ronny stopped short of drawing his gun only by a fraction when half drunken demonstraters stopped them.

The driver, a wispy, sad looking type, shook his head. "There's no going back now," he told them over his shoulder.

"No going back. Last week I was all with the rest—I never did believe David the One was really immortal. But you was just used to idea, see? It'd always been that way, with the priests running everything and we was used to it. Now I wish we was still that way. At least you knew how you stood, see? Now, what's going to happen?"

"That's an interesting question," Tog said politely.

Ronny said, "Possibly you'll have the chance to build a better world, now."

The driver shot a contemptuous look over his shoulder. "Better world? What do I want with a better world? I just don't want to be bothered. I've been getting my three squares a day, got a nice little flat for my family. How do I know it's not going to be a worse world?"

"That's always a possibility," Tog told him. "Do most people seem to feel the same?"

"Practically everybody I know does," he said glumly. "But the fat's in the fire now. The priests are trying to hold on, but their government is falling apart all over the place."

"Well," Ronny said, "at least you can figure just about anything in the way of a new government will be better than one based on superstition and inquisition. It couldn't get worse."

"Things can always get worse," the other contradicted him sadly.

They left the cab before an impressively tall, many windowed building in city center. As they mounted the steps, Ronny frowned at her. "You seemed to be encouraging that man in his pessimism. So far as I can see, the best thing that ever happened to this planet was toppling that phony priesthood."

"Perhaps," she said agreeably. "However, the man's mind was an ossified one. A surprisingly large percentage of people have them, especially when it comes to institutions such as religion and government. We weren't going to be able to teach him anything, but it was possible to learn from him."

Ronny grunted his disgust. "What could we possibly learn from him?"

Tog said mildly, "We could learn what people of the street were thinking. It might give us some ideas about what direction the new government will take."

They approached the portals of the building and were halted by an armed Space Forces guard of half a dozen men. Their sergeant saluted, taking in their obvious other-planet clothing.

"Identifications, please," he said briskly.

They showed their badges and were passed on through. Ronny said to him, "Much trouble, sergeant?"

The other shrugged. "No. Just precautions, sir. We've been here only three or four weeks. Civil disturbance. We're used to it. Were over on Montezuma two basic months ago. Now, there was *real* trouble. Had to shoot our way out."

Tog called, "Coming, Ronny? I have this elevator waiting."

He followed her, scowling. An idea was trying to work its way through. Somehow he missed getting it.

Headquarters of the Department of Justice were on the eighth floor. A receptionist clerk led them through three or four doors to the single office which housed Section G.

A red eyed, exhausted agent looked up from the sole desk and snarled a question at them. Ronny didn't get it, but Tog said mildly, "Probationary Agent Ronald Bronston and Tog Lee Chang Chu. On special assignment." She flicked open her badge so that the other could see it.

His manner changed. "Sorry," he said, getting up to shake hands. "I'm Mouley Hassan, in charge of Section G on New Delos. We've just had a crisis here, as you can imagine. The worst of it's now over." He added sourly, "I hope. All my assistants have already taken off for Avalon." He was a short statured, dark complected man, his features betraying his Semitic background.

Ronny shook hands with him and said, "Sorry to bother you at a time like this."

They found chairs and Mouley Hassan flicked a key on his order box and said to them, "How about a drink? They make a wonderful sparkling wine on this planet. Trust any theocracy to have top potables."

46

Ronny accepted the offer; Tog refused it politely. She sat demurely, her hands in her lap.

Mouley Hassan ran a weary hand through already mussed hair. "What's this special assignment you're on?"

Ronny said, "Commissioner Metaxa has sent me looking for Tommy Paine."

"Tommy Paine!" the other blurted. "At a time like this, when I haven't had three nights' sleep in the last three hectic weeks, you come around looking for Tommy Paine?"

Ronny was taken aback. "Sid Jakes seemed to think this might be one of Paine's jobs."

Tog said mildly, "What better place to look for Tommy Paine than in a situation like this, Agent Hassan?" Her eyebrows went up. "Or don't you think the quest for Paine is an important one?"

The other subsided somewhat. "I suppose you're right," he said. "I'm deathly tired. Do whatever you want. But don't expect much from me."

Tog said—just a trifle tartly, Ronny thought—"We'll have to call on you, as usual, Agent Hassan. There's probably no single job in Section G more important than the pursuit of Tommy Paine."

"All right, all right," Mouley Hassan said. "I'll coöperate. How long have you been away from Earth?" he asked Ronny.

"About one basic week."

"Oh," he grunted. "This is your first stop, eh? Well, I don't envy you your job." He brought a cool bottle from a delivery-drawer in the desk along with two glasses. "Here's the wine."

Ronny leaned forward to accept the glass. "This situation here," he said, "do you think it can be laid to Paine?"

Mouley Hassan shrugged wearily. "I don't know."

Ronny sipped the drink, looking at the tired agent over the glass rim. "From what we understand, check has been kept on all persons leaving the planet since the bombing."

"Check is right. There's only one ship that took off, and it carried nobody except my assistants. If you ask me, I still needed them, but some brass hat back on Earth decided they were more necessary over on Avalon." He was disgusted.

Ronny put the glass down. "You mean only one ship's left this planet since the God-King was killed?"

"That's right. It was like pulling teeth to get the visas."

"How many men aboard?"

Mouley Hassan looked at him speculatively. "Four-man crew and six Section G operatives."

Tog said brightly, "Why, that means, then, that either Tommy Paine is still on this planet, or he's one of the passengers or crew members of that ship." She added, "That is, of course, unless he had a private craft, hidden away somewhere."

Ronny slumped back into his chair as some of the ramifications came home to him. "If it was Tommy Paine at all," he said.

Mouley Hassan nodded. "That's always a point." He finished his glass and looked pleadingly at Tog. "Look, I have work. If I can finish some of it, I might have time for some sleep. Couldn't we postpone the search for Tommy Paine?"

Tog said nothing to him.

Ronny came to his feet. "We'll get along. A couple of ideas occur to me. I'll check with you later."

"Fine," the agent said. He shook hands with them again. He said, somehow more to Tog than to Ronny, "I know how important your job is. It's just that I've been pushed to the point where I can't operate efficiently."

She smiled her understanding, and gave him her small, delicate hand.

In the elevator, Ronny said to her, "Why should this sort of thing particularly affect Section G?"

Tog said, "It's times like this that planets drop out of the UP. Or, possibly, get into the hands of some jingoistic military group and start off halfcocked to provoke a war with some other planet, or to missionarize or propagandize it." She thought about it a moment. "A new revolution, in government or religion, seems almost invariably to want to spread the light. An absolute compulsion to bring to others the new truths that they've found." She added, her voice holding a trace of mockery, "Usually the new truths are rather hoary ones, and there are few interested in hearing them."

VIII

THEY SPENT their first day in getting accommodations in a centrally located hotel, in making arrangements, through the Department of Justice, for the local means of exchange—it turned out to be coinage, based on gold—and getting the feel of their surroundings.

Evidently Delos, the capital city of the planet New Delos, was but slowly emerging from the chaos that had followed the assassination. A provisional government, composed of representatives of half a dozen different organizations which had sprung up like mushrooms following the collapse of the regime, had assumed power. Elections had been promised and were to be brought off when arrangements could be made.

Meanwhile, the actual government was still largely in the hands of the lower echelons of the priesthood. A nervous priesthood it was, seemingly desirous of getting out from under while the getting was good, afraid of being held responsible for former excesses.

Ronny Bronston, high hopes still in his head, looked up the Sub-Bishop who had given them landing orders while they'd still been aboard the Space Forces cruiser. Tog was off making arrangements for various details involved in their being in Delos in its time of crisis.

A dozen times, on his way over to keep his appointment with the official, Ronny had to step into doorways or in other ways make himself inconspicuous. Gangs of demonstrators roamed the street, some of them drunken, looking for trouble, and scornful of police or the military. Twice, when it looked as though he might be roughed up, Ronny drew his gun and held it in open sight, ready for use, but not threateningly. The demonstrators made off.

49

His throat was dry by the time he reached his destination. The life of a Section G agent, on interplanetary assignment, had its drawbacks.

The Sub-Bishop had formerly been in charge of Interplanetary Communications which involved commerce as well as intercourse with United Planets. It must have been an ultra-responsible position only a month ago. Now his offices were all but deserted.

He looked at Ronny's badge, only vaguely interested. "Section G of the Bureau of Investigation," he said. "I don't believe I am aware of your responsibilities. However," he nodded with sour courtesy, "please be seated. You must forgive my lack of ability to offer refreshment. Isn't there an old tradition about rats deserting a sinking ship? I am afraid my former assistants had rodentlike instincts."

Ronny said, "Section G deals with Interplanetary Security, sir—"

"I am addressed as Holiness," the other said.

Ronny looked at him. "Sorry," he said. "I am a citizen of the United Planets, not any one planet, even Earth. UP citizens have complete religious freedom. In my case I am unaffiliated with any church."

The Sub-Bishop let it pass. He said sourly, "I am afraid that even here on New Delos, I am seldom honored by my title any more. Go on, you say you deal with Interplanetary Security."

"That's correct. In cases like this we're interested in checking to see if there is any possibility that citizens other than New Delos are involved in your internal affairs."

The other's eyes were suddenly slits. He said, heavily, "You suspect that David the One was assassinated by an alien?"

Ronny had to tread carefully here. "I make no such suggestion. I am merely here to check on the possibility. If such was the case, my duty would be to arrest the man, or men."

"If we got hold of him, you'd have small chance of asserting your authority," the priest growled. "What did you want to know?"

"I understand that no interplanetary craft have left New Delos since the assassination."

"None except a United Planets ship which was carefully inspected."

Ronny said tightly, "But what facilities do you have to check on secret spaceports, possibly located in some remote desert or mountain area?"

The New Delian laughed sourly. "There is no other planet in all the United Planets with our degree of security. We even imported the most recent developments in artificial satellites equipped with the most delicate of detection devices. I assure you, it is utterly impossible for a spacecraft to land or take off from New Delos without our knowledge."

Ronny Bronston's eyes lit with excitement. "These security measures of yours. To what extent do you keep under observation all aliens on the planet?"

The priest's chuckle had a nasty quality. "You are quite ignorant of our institutions, evidently. Every person on New Delos, in every way of life, was under constant survey from the cradle to the grave. Aliens were highly discouraged. When they appeared on New Delos at all, they were restricted in their movements to this, our capital city."

Ronny let air whistle from his lungs. "Then," he said triumphantly, "if any alien had anything to do with this, he is still on the planet. Can you get me a list of all aliens?"

The other laughed again, still sourly. "But there are none. None except you employees of United Planets. I'm afraid you're on a wild-goose chase."

Ronny stared at him blankly. "But commercial representatives, cultural exchange—"

The priest said flatly, "No. None at all. All commerce was handled through UP. We encouraged no cultural exchanges. We wished to keep our people uncorrupted. United Planets alone had the right to land on our one spaceport."

The Section G agent came to his feet. This was much simpler than he could ever have hoped for. He thanked the other, but avoided the necessity of shaking hands, and left.

He found a helio-cab and dialed it to the UP building, finding strange the necessity of slipping coins into the vehicle's slots until the correct amount for his destination had been deposited. Coinage was no longer in use on Earth.

At the UP building he retraced his steps of the day before to the single office of Section G.

To his surprise, not only Mouley Hassan was there, but Tog as well. Hassan had evidently had at least a few hours of sleep. He was in better shape.

They exchanged the usual amenities and took their chairs again.

Hassen said, "We were just gossiping. It's been years since I've been in Greater Washington. Lee Chang tells me that Sid Jakes is now a Supervisor. I worked with him for awhile, when I first joined Section G. How about a glass of wine?"

Ronny said, "Look. If Tommy Paine was connected with this, and it's almost positive he was, we've got him."

The others looked at him.

"You've evidently been busy," Tog said mildly.

He turned to her. "He's trapped, Tog! He can't get off the planet."

Mouley Hassan rubbed a hand through his hair. "It'd be hard, all right. They've got the people under rein here such as you've never seen before. Or they did until this blew up."

Ronny sketched the situation to Tog, winding up with, "The only thing that makes sense is that it's a Tommy Paine job. The local citizens would never have been able to get their hands on such a bomb, or been able to have made the arrangements for its delivery. They're under too much surveillance."

Tog said thoughtfully. "But how did he escape all this surveillance?"

"Don't you understand? He's working here, in this building, as an employee of UP. There is no other alternative."

They stared at him.

"I think perhaps you're right," Tog said finally.

Ronny turned to Mouley Hassan. "Can you get a list of all UP employees?"

"Of course." He flicked his order box, barked a command into it.

Ronny said, "It's going to be a matter of eliminating the impossible. For instance, what is the earliest known case of Tommy Paine's activity?"

Tog thought back. "So far as we know definitely, about twenty-two years ago."

"Fine," Ronny said, increasingly excited. "That will eliminate all persons less than, say, forty years of age. We can assume he was at least twenty when he began."

Hassan said, "Can we eliminate all women employees?"

Ronny said. "I'd think so. The few times he's been seen, all reports are of a man. And that case on the planet Mother where he put himself over as a Holy Man. He could hardly have been a woman in disguise in a Stone Age culture such as that."

Hassan said, "And this Tommy Paine has been flitting around this part of the galaxy for years, so anyone who has been here steadily for a period of even a couple of years or so can't be suspect."

Mouley Hassan thrust his hand into a delivery drawer and brought forth a handful of punched cards, possibly fifty in all.

"Surely there's more people than that working in this building," Ronny protested.

Mouley Hassan said, "No. I've already eliminated everyone who is a citizen of New Delos. Obviously, Tommy Paine is an alien. We have only forty-eight Earthlings and other United Planets citizens working here."

He carried the cards to a small collator and worked for a moment on its controls, as Tog and Ronny watched him with mounting tension. "Let's see," he muttered. "We eliminate all women, all those less than forty, all who haven't done a great deal of travel, those who have been here for several years."

The end of it was that they eliminated everyone employed in the UP building.

The cards were stacked back on Mouley Hassan's desk

again, and the three of them sat around and looked glumly
at them.

Ronny said, "He's tinkered with the files. He counter-
feited fake papers for himself, or something. Possibly he's
pulled his own card and it isn't in this stack you have."

Mouley Hassan said, "We'll doublecheck all those possibilities, but you're wrong. Possibly a few hundred years ago,
but not today. Forgery and counterfeiting are things of the
past. And, believe me, the Bureau of Investigation, and
especially Section G, may seem to be on the slipshod side,
but they aren't. We're not going to find anything wrong with
those cards. Tommy Paine simply is not working for UP on
New Delos."

"Then," Ronny said, "there's only one alternative. He's on
this UP ship going to . . . what was the name of its destination?"

"Avalon," Mouley Hassan said, his face thoughtful.

Tog said, "Do you have any ideas on the men aboard?"

Mouley Hassan said, "There were four crewmen, and six
of our agents."

Tog said, "Unless one of them has faked papers, the six
agents are eliminated. That leaves the crew members. Do
you know anything about them?"

Hassan shook his head.

Ronny said, "Let's communicate with Avalon. Tell our
representatives there to be sure that none of the occupants
of that ship leaves Avalon until we get there."

Mouley Hassan said, "Good idea." He turned to his
screen and said into it, "Section G, Bureau of Investigation,
on the Planet Avalon."

In a moment the screen lit up. An elderly agent, as Section G agents seemed to go, looked up at them. Mouley
Hassan held his silver badge so the other could see it and on
the Avalon agent's nod said, "I'm Hassan from New Delos.
We've just had a crisis here and there seems to be a chance
that it's a Tommy Paine job. Agent Bronston here is on an
assignment tracking him down. I'll turn it over to Bronston."

The Avalon agent nodded again, and looked at Ronny.

Ronny said urgently, "We don't have the time to give you details, but every indication is that Paine is on a UP spacecraft with Avalon as its destination. There are only ten men aboard, and six of them are Section G operatives."

The other pursed his lips. "I see. You think you have the old fox cornered, eh?"

"Possibly," Ronny said. "There are various ifs. Miss Tog and I can doublecheck here. Then, as soon as we can clear exit visas, we'll start for Avalon immediately."

The Avalon Section G agent said, "I haven't the authority to control the movements of other agents—they have as high ranks as I have." Then he added, expressionlessly, "And probably higher than yours, too."

Ronny said, "But the four-man crew?"

The other said, "These men are coming to Avalon to work on a job that will take at least six months. We'll make a routine check, and I'll try and make sure the whole ten will still be on Avalon when and if you arrive."

They had to be satisfied with that.

IX

THEY CHECKED all ways from the middle, nor did it take long. There was no doubt. If this had been a Tommy Paine job, and it almost surely had, then there was only one way in which he could have escaped from the planet and that was by the single spacecraft that had left, destination Avalon. He was not *on* the planet—that was definite, Ronny felt. A stranger on New Delos was as conspicuous as a walrus in a goldfish bowl. There simply were no such.

They spent most of their time checking and rechecking United Planets personnel, but there was no question there either.

Mouley Hassan and others of UP personnel helped cut the red tape involved in getting exit visas from New Delos. It wasn't as complicated as it might have been a week or two before. No one seemed to be so confident of his

authority in the new provisional government that he dared
veto a United Planets request.

Mouley Hassan was able to arrange for a small space
yacht, slower than a military craft, but capable of getting
them to Avalon in a few days time. A one-man crew was
sufficient; Ronny, and especially Tog, could spell him on the
watches.

Time aboard was spent largely in studying up on Avalon,
going over and over again anything known about the elusive
Tommy Paine, and playing Battle Chess and bickering with
Tog Lee Chang Chu.

If it hadn't been for this ability to argue against just about
anything Ronny managed to say, he could have been at-
tracted to her to the detriment of the job. She was a good
traveler, which few people are; she was an ultra-efficient
assistant; she was a joy to look at; and she never intruded.
But, good God, how the woman could bicker!

The two of them were studying in the ship's luxurious
lounge when Ronny looked up and said, "Do you have any
idea why those six agents were sent to Avalon?"

"No," she said.

He indicated the booklet he was reading. "From what I
can see here, it sounds like one of the most advanced planets
in the UP. They've made some of the most useful advances
in industrial techniques of the past century."

"Oh, I don't know," Tog mused. "I don't have much regard for Industrial Feudalism, myself. It starts off with a
bang, but tends to go sterile."

"Industrial feudalism," he said indignantly. "What do you
mean? The government is a constitutional monarchy with
the king merely a powerless symbol. The standard of living
is high. Elections are honest and democratic. They've got a
three-party system . . ."

"Which is largely phony," Tog interrupted. "You've got to
do some reading between the lines, especially when the
books you're reading are turned out by the industrial feudalistic publishing companies in Avalon."

"What's this industrial feudalism you keep talking about? Avalon has a system of free enterprise."

"A gobbledygook term," Tog said. "Industrial feudalism is a socio-economic system that develops when industrial wealth is concentrated into the hands of a comparatively few families. It finally gets to the point of a closed circle all but impossible to break into. These industrial feudalistic families become so powerful that only in rare instances can anyone lift himself into their society. They dominate every field, including the so-called labor unions, which amount to one of the biggest businesses of all. With their unlimited resources they even own every means of dispensing information."

"You mean," Ronny argued, "that on Avalon you can't start up a newspaper of your own and say whatever you wish?"

"Certainly you can, theoretically. If you have the resources. Unfortunately, such enterprises become increasingly expensive to start. Or you could start a radio, TV or Tri-D station—if you had the resources. However, even if you overcame all your handicaps and your newspaper or broadcasting station became a success, the industrial feudalistic families in control of Avalon's publishing and broadcasting fields have the endless resources to buy you out, or squeeze you out, by one nasty means or another."

Ronny snorted. "Well, the people must be satisfied or they'd vote some fundamental changes."

Tog nodded. "They're satisfied, and no wonder. Since childhood every means of forming their opinions has been in the hands of industrial feudalistic families—including the schools."

"You mean the schools are private?"

"No, they don't have to be. The government is completely dominated by the fifty or so families which for all practical purposes own Avalon. That includes the schools. Some of the higher institutions of learning are private, but they, too, are largely dependent upon grants from the families."

Ronny was irritated by her know it all air. He tapped the book he'd been reading with a finger. "They don't control the government. Avalon's got a three-party system. Any time the people don't like the government, they can vote in an alternative."

"That's an optical illusion. There are three parties, but each is dominated by the fifty families, and election laws are such that for all practical purposes it's impossible to start another party. Theoretically it's possible; actually it isn't. The voters can vary back and forth between the three political parties but it doesn't make any difference which one they elect. They all stand for the same thing—a continuation of the status quo."

"Then you claim it isn't democracy at all?"

Tog sighed. "That's a much abused word. Actually, pure democracy is seldom seen. They pretty well had it in primitive society where government was based on the family. You voted for one of your relatives in your clan to represent you in the tribal councils. Everyone in the tribe was equal so far as apportionments of the necessities of life were concerned. No one, not even a tribal chief, was better than anyone else, and no one had a better home."

Ronny said, snappishly, "And if man had remained at that level, we'd never have gotten anywhere."

"That's right," she said. "For progress, man needed a leisure class. Somebody with the time to study, to experiment, to work things out."

He said, "We're getting away from the point. You said in spite of appearances they don't have democracy on Avalon."

"They have a pretense of it. But only free men can practice democracy. So long as your food, clothing and shelter are controlled by someone else, you aren't free. Wait until I think of an example." She put her right forefinger to her chin, thoughtfully.

Ye gods, she was a doll. If only she weren't so confounded irritating.

Tog said, "Do you remember the State of California in Earth history?"

"I think so. On the west coast of North America."

58

"That's right. Well, back in the Twentieth Century, Christian calendar, they had an economic depression. During it a crackpot organization called Thirty Dollars Every Thursday managed to get itself on the ballot. Times were bad enough, but if this particular bunch had got into power it would have become chaotic. At first no thinking person took them seriously; however, a majority of people in California at that time had little to lose and in the final week or so of the election campaign the polls showed that Thirty Dollars Every Thursday was going to win. So, a few days before voting many of the larger industries and businesses in the State ran full page ads in the newspapers. They said substantially the same thing. *If Thirty Dollars Every Thursday wins this election, our concern will close its doors. Do not bother to come back to work Monday.*"

Ronny was scowling at her. "What's your point?"

She shrugged delicate shoulders. "The crackpots were defeated, of course, which was actually good for California. But my point is that the voters of California were not truly free since their livelihoods were controlled by others. This is an extreme case, of course, but the fact always applies."

A thought suddenly hit Ronny Bronston. "Look," he said. "Tommy Paine. Do you think he's merely escaping from New Delos, or is it possible that Avalon is his next destination? Is he going to try and overthrow the government there?"

She was shaking her head, but frowning. "I don't think so. Things are quite stable on Avalon."

"Stable?" he scowled at her. "From what you've just been saying, they're pretty bad."

She continued to shake her head. "Don't misunderstand, Ronny. On an assignment like this, it's easy to get the impression that all the United Planets are in a state of sociopolitical confusion, but it isn't so. A small minority of planets are ripe for the sort of trouble Tommy Paine stirs up. Most are working away, developing, making progress, slowly evolving. Avalon is one of these. The way things are there, Tommy Paine couldn't make a dent on changing things, even

59

if he wanted to, and there's no particular reason to believe he does."

Ronny growled. "From what I can learn of the guy he's anxious to stir up trouble wherever he goes."

"I don't know. If there's any pattern at all in his activities, it seems to be that he picks spots where things are ripe to boil over on their own. He acts as a catalyst. In a place like Avalon he wouldn't get to first base. Possibly fifty years from now things will have developed on Avalon to the point where there is dissatisfaction. By that time," she said dryly, "we'll assume Tommy Paine will no longer be a problem to the Commissariat of Interplanetary Affairs for one reason or the other."

Ronny took up his book again. He growled, "I can't figure out his motivation. If I could just put my finger on that."

For once she agreed with him. "I've got an idea, Ronny, that once you have that, you'll have Tommy Paine."

X

THEY DREW a blank on Avalon.

Or, at least, it was drawn for them before they ever arrived.

The Section G agent permanently assigned to that planet had already checked and doublechecked the possibilities. None of the four-man crew of the UP spacecraft had been on New Delos at the time of the assassination of the God-King. They, and their craft, had been light-years away on another job.

Ronny Bronston couldn't believe it.

The older agent—his name was Jheru Bulchand—was definite. He went over it with Ronny and Tog in a bar adjoining UP headquarters. He had dossiers on each of the ten men—detailed dossiers. On the face of it, none of them could be Paine.

"But one of them *has* to be," Ronny pleaded. He explained their method of eliminating the forty-eight employees of UP on New Delos.

Bulchand shrugged. "You've got holes in that method of elimination. You're assuming Tommy Paine is an individual, and you have no reason to. My own theory is that it's an organization."

Ronny said unhappily, "Then you're of the opinion that there is a Tommy Paine?"

The older agent was puffing comfortably on an old style briar pipe. He nodded definitely. "I believe Tommy Paine exists as an organization. Possibly once, originally, it was a single person, but now it's a group. How large, I wouldn't know. Probably not too large or by this time somebody would have cracked and we would have caught them. Catch one and you've got the whole organization, what with our modern means of interrogation."

Tog said, "I've heard the opinion before."

Jheru Bulchand pointed at Ronny with his pipe stem. "If it's an organization, then none of that eliminating you did is valid. Your assassin could have been one of the women. He could have been one of the men you eliminated as too young —someone recently admitted to the Tommy Paine organization."

Ronny checked the last of his theories. "Why did Section G send six of its agents here?"

"Nothing to do with Tommy Paine," Bulchand said. "It's a different sort of crisis."

"Just for my own satisfaction, what kind of crisis?"

Bulchand sketched it quickly. "There are two Earth type planets in this solar system. Avalon was the first to be colonized, and it developed rapidly. After a couple of centuries, Avalonians went over and settled on Catalina. They eventually set up a government of their own. Now, Avalon has a surplus of industrial products. Her economic system is such that she produces more than she can sell back to her own people. There's a glut."

Tog said demurely, "So, of course, they want to dump it in Catalina."

61

Bulchand nodded. "In fact, they're willing to give it away. They've offered to build railroads, turn over ships and aircraft, donate whole factories to Catalina's slowly developing economy."

Ronny said, "Well, how does that call for Section G agents?"

"Catalina has evoked Article Two of the UP Charter. No member planet of UP is to interfere with the internal political, socio-economic or religious affairs of another member planet. Avalon claims the Charter doesn't apply since Catalina belongs to the same solar system and since she's a former colony. We're trying to smooth the whole thing over, before Avalon dreams up some excuse for military action."

Ronny stared at him. "I get the feeling every other sentence is being left out of your explanation. It just doesn't make sense. In the first place, why is Avalon as anxious as all that to give away what sounds like a fantastic amount of goods?"

"I told you, they have a glut. They've overproduced and, as a result, they've got a king-size depression on their hands, or will have unless they find markets."

"Well, why not trade with some of the planets that want their products?"

Tog said as though reasoning with a youngster, "Planets outside their own solar system are too far away for it to be practical even if the Avalonians had commodities they didn't. They need a nearby planet more backward than Avalon—a planet like Catalina."

"Well, that brings us to the more fantastic question. Why in the world doesn't Catalina accept? It sounds to me like pure philanthropy on the part of Avalon."

Bulchand was wagging his pipe stem in a negative gesture. "Bronston, governments are never motivated by idealistic reasons. Individuals might be, and even small groups, but governments never. Governments, including that of Avalon, exist for the benefit of the class or classes that control them. The only things that motivate them are the interests of that class."

"Well, this sounds like an exception," Ronny said argumentatively. "How can Catalina lose if the Avalonians grant them railroads, factories and all the rest of it?"

Tog said, "Don't you see, Ronny? It gives Avalon a foothold in the Catalina economy. When the locomotives wear out on the railroad, new engines, new parts, will have to be purchased. They won't be available on Catalina because there will be no railroad industry because none will ever have grown up. Catalina manufacturers couldn't compete with that initial free gift. They'll be dependent on Avalon for future equipment. In the factories, when machines wear out, they will be replaceable only with the products of Avalon's industry."

Bulchand said, "There's an analogy in the early history of the United States. When its fledgling steel industry began, they set up a high tariff to protect it against British competition. The British were amazed and indignant, pointing out that they could sell American steel products at one third the local prices, if only allowed to do so. The United States said no thanks, it didn't want to be tied, industrially, to Great Britain's apron strings. And in a couple of decades American steel production passed England's. In a couple of more decades American steel production was many times that of England's and she was taking British markets away from her all over the globe."

"At any rate," Ronny said, "it's not a Tommy Paine matter."

Just for luck, though, Ronny and Tog doublechecked all over again on Bulchand's efforts. They interviewed all six of the Section G agents. Each of them carried a silver badge that gleamed only for the individual who possessed it. All of which eliminated the possibility that Paine had assumed the identity of a Section G operative. So that was out.

They checked the four crew members, but there was no doubt there, either. The craft had been far away at the time of the assassination on New Delos.

On the third day, Ronny Bronston, disgusted, knocked on the door of Tog's hotel room. The door screen lit up and Tog,

63

looking out at him, said, "Oh, come on in, Ronny, I was just talking to Earth."

He entered.

Tog had set up her Section G communicator on a desk top and Sid Jakes' grinning face was in the tiny, brilliant screen. Ronny approached close enough for the other to take him in.

Jakes said happily, "Hi, Ronny. No luck, eh?"

Ronny shook his head, trying not to let his face betray his feelings of defeat. This after all was a probationary assignment, and the supervisor had the power to send Ronny Bronston back to the drudgery of his office job at Population Statistics.

"Still working on it. I suppose it's a matter of returning to New Delos and grinding away at the forty-eight employees of the UP there."

Sid Jakes pursed his lips. "I don't know. Possibly this whole thing was a false alarm. At any rate, there seems to be a hotter case on the fire. If our local agents have it straight, Paine is about to pull one of his coups on Kropotkin. This is a top top-secret, of course—one of the few times we've ever detected him before the act."

Ronny was suddenly alert, his fatigue of a moment ago completely forgotten. "Where?" he said.

"Kropotkin," Jakes said. "One of the most backward planets in UP and seemingly a setup for Paine's sort of trouble making. The authorities, if you can use the term applied to Kropotkin, are already complaining, threatening to invoke Article One of the Charter, or to resign from UP." Jakes looked at Tog again. "Do you know Kropotkin, Lee Chang?"

She shook her head. "I've heard of it, rather vaguely. Named after some old anarchist, I believe."

"That's the place. One of the few anarchist societies in UP. You don't hear much from them." He turned to Ronny again. "I think that's your bet. Hop to it, boy. We're going to catch this Tommy Paine guy, or organization, or whatever, soon or United Planets is going to know it. We can't keep the lid on indefinitely. If word gets around of his activities, then we'll lose member planets like Christmas trees shedding needles after New Year's." He grinned widely. "That sounds like a neat trick, eh?"

XI

RONNY BRONSTON HAD got to the point where he avoided controversial subjects with Tog even when provoked, and she had a sneaky little way of provoking arguments. They had only one real verbal battle on the way to Kropotkin.

It had started innocently enough after dinner on the space liner on which they had taken passage for the first part of the trip. To kill time they were playing Battle Chess with its larger board and added contingents of pawns and castles.

Ronny said idly, "You know, in spite of the fact that I'm a third generation United Planets citizen and employee, I'm just beginning to realize how far out some of our member planets are. I had no idea before."

She frowned in concentration, before moving. She was advancing her men in echelon attack, taking losses in exchange for territory and trying to pen him up in such small space that he couldn't maneuver.

She said, "How do you mean?"

Ronny lifted and dropped a shoulder. "Well, New Delos and its theocracy, for instance, and Shangri-La and Mother and some of the other planets with extremes in government or socio-economic system. I hadn't the vaguest idea about such places."

She made a deprecating sound. "You should see Amazonia, or, for that matter, the Orwellian State."

"*Amazonia*," he said. "Does that mean what it sounds like it does?"

She made her move and settled back in satisfaction. Her pawns were in such position that his bishops were both unusable. He'd tried to play a phalanx game in the early stages of her attack, but she'd broken through, rolling up his left flank after sacrificing a castle and knight.

"Certainly does," she said. "A fairly recently colonized planet. A few thousand feminists—no men at all—moved onto it a few centuries ago. And it's still an out and out matriarchy."

Ronny cleared his throat delicately. "Without men . . . ah, how did they continue several centuries?"

Tog suppressed her amusement. "Artificial insemination, at first, so I understand. They brought their supply with them. But then there were boys among the first generation on the new planet and even the Amazonians weren't up to cold bloodedly butchering their children. So they merely enslaved them. Nice girls."

Ronny stared at her. "You mean all men are automatically slaves on this planet?"

"That's right."

Ronny made an improperly thought out move, trying to bring up a castle to reinforce his collapsing flank. He said, "UP allows *anybody* to join, evidently," and there was disgust in his voice.

"Why not?" she said mildly.

"Well, there should be *some* standards."

Tog moved quickly, dominating with a knight several squares he couldn't afford to lose. She looked up at him, her dark eyes sparking. "The point of UP is to include all the planets. That way at least conflict can be avoided and some exchange of science, industrial techniques and cultural gains take place. And you must remember that while in power practically no socio-economic system will admit to the fact that it could possibly change for the better. But actually there is nothing less stable. Socio-economic systems are almost always in a condition of flux. Planets such as Amazonia might for a time seem so brutal in their methods as to exclude their right to civilized intercourse with the rest. However, one of these days there'll be a change—or one of these centuries. They all change, sooner or later." She added softly, "Even Han."

"Han?" Ronny said.

Her voice was quiet. "Where I was born, Ronny. Colonized from China in the very early days. In fact, I spent my childhood in a commune." She said musingly, "The party bureaucrats thought their system was an impregnable, unchangeable one. Your move."

Ronny was fascinated. "And what happened?" He was in full retreat now, and with nowhere to go, his pieces pinned up for the slaughter. He moved a pawn to try and open up his queen.

"Why don't you concede?" she said. "Tommy Paine happened."

"Paine!"

"Uh-huh. It's a long story. I'll tell you about it sometime." She pressed closer with her own queen.

He stared disgustedly at the board. "Well, that's what I mean," he muttered. "I had no idea there were so many varieties of crackpot politico-economic systems among the UP membership."

"They're not necessarily crackpot," she protested mildly. "Just at different stages of development."

"Not crackpot!" he said. "Here we are heading for a planet named Kropotkin which evidently practices anarchy."

"Your move," she said. "What's wrong with anarchism?"

He glowered at her, in outraged disgust. Was it absolutely impossible for him to say anything without her disagreement?

Tog said mildly, "The anarchistic ethic is one of the highest man has ever developed." She added, after a moment of pretty consideration, "Unfortunately, it hasn't been practical to put it into practice. It will be interesting to see how they've done on Kropotkin."

"Anarchist ethic, yet," Ronny snapped. "I'm no student of the movement, but the way I understand it, there isn't any."

Tog smiled sweetly. "The belief upon which they base their teachings is that no man is capable of judging another."

Ronny cast his eyes ceilingward. "O.K., I give up!"

She began rapidly resetting the pieces. "Another game?" she said brightly.

67

"Hey! I didn't mean the game! I was just about to counter-attack."

"Ha!" she said.

XII

THE SECTION G agent on Kropotkin was named Hideka Ya-mamoto, but he was on a field tour and wouldn't be back for several days. However, there wasn't especially any great hurry so far as Ronny Bronston and Tog Lee Chang Chu knew. They got themselves organized in the rather rustic equivalent of a hotel, which was located fairly near UP headquarters, and took up the usual problems of arranging for local exchange, meals, means of transportation and such necessities.

It was a greater problem than usual. In fact, if it hadn't been for the presence of the UP organization, which had already gone through all this the hard way, some of the difficulties would have been all but insurmountable.

For instance, there was no local exchange. There was no medium of exchange at all. Evidently simple barter was the rule.

In the hotel—if it could be called a hotel—lobby, Ronny Bronston looked at Tog. "Anarchism!" he said. "Oh, great. The highest ethic of all. And what's the means of transportation on this wonderful planet? The horse. And how are we going to get a couple of horses with no means of exchange?"

She tinkled laughter.

"All right," he said. "You're the Man Friday. You find out the details and handle them. I'm going out to take a look around the town—if you can call this a town."

"It's the capital of Kropotkin," Tog said placatingly, though with a mocking background in her tone. "Name of Bakunin. And very pleasant, too, from what little I've seen. Not a bit of smog, industrial fumes, street dirt, street noises—"

"How could there be?" he injected disgustedly. "There isn't any industry, there aren't any cars, and for all practical

68

purposes, no streets. The houses are a quarter of a mile or so apart."

She laughed at him again. "City boy," she said. "Go on out there and enjoy nature a little. It'll do you good. Anybody who has cooped himself up in that one big city, Earth, all his life ought to enjoy seeing what the great outdoors looks like."

He looked at her and grinned. She was cute as a pixie, and there were no two ways about that. He wondered for a moment what kind of a wife she'd make. And then shuddered inwardly. Life would be one big contradiction of anything he managed to get out of his trap.

He strolled idly along what was little more than a country path and it came to him that there were probably few worlds in the whole UP where he'd have been prone to do this within the first few hours he'd been on the planet. He would have been afraid, elsewhere, of anything from footpads to police, from unknown vehicles to unknown traffic laws. There was something bewildering about being an Earthling and being set down suddenly in New Delos or on Avalon.

Here, somehow, he already had a feeling of peace.

Evidently, although Bakunin was supposedly a city, its populace tilled their fields and provided themselves with their own food. He could see no signs of stores or warehouses. And the UP building, which was no great edifice itself, was the only thing in town which looked even remotely like a governmental building.

He approached one of the wooden houses. The thing would have been priceless on Earth as an antique to be erected as a museum in some crowded park. For that matter, it would have been priceless for the wood it contained. Evidently the planet Kropotkin still had considerable virgin forest.

An old-timer, smoking a pipe, sat on the cottage's front steps. He nodded politely.

Ronny stopped. He might as well try to get a little of the feel of the place. He said courteously, "A pleasant evening."

69

The old-timer nodded. "As evenings should be after a fruitful day's toil. Sit down, comrade. You must be from the United Planets. Have you ever seen Earth?"

Ronny accepted the invitation and felt a soothing calm descend upon him almost immediately. An almost disturbingly pleasant calm. He said, "I was born on·Earth."

"Ai?" the old man said. "Tell me. The books say that Kropotkin is an Earth type planet within what they call a few degrees. But is it? Is Kropotkin truly like the mother planet?"

Ronny looked about him. He'd seen some of this world as the shuttle rocket had brought them down from the passing liner. The forests, the lakes, the rivers, and the great sections untouched by man's hands. Now he saw the areas between homes, the neat fields, the signs of human toil—the toil of hands, not machines.

"No," he said, shaking his head. "I'm afraid not. This is how Earth must have been once. But no longer."

The other nodded. "Our total population is but a few million," he said. Then, "I would like to see the mother planet, but I suppose I never shall."

Ronny said diplomatically, "I have seen little of Kropotkin thus far but I am not so sure but that I might not be happy to stay here, rather than ever return to Earth."

The old man knocked the ashes from his pipe by striking it against the heel of a work-gnarled hand. He looked about him thoughtfully and said, "Yes, perhaps you're right. I am an old man and life has been good. I suppose I should be glad that I'll unlikely live to see Kropotkin change."

"Change? You plan changes?"

The old man looked at him and there seemed to be a very faint bitterness, politely suppressed. "I wouldn't say *we* planned them, comrade. Certainly not we of the older generation. But the trend toward change is already to be seen by anyone who wishes to look, and our institutions won't long be able to stand. But, of course, if you're from United Planets you would know more of this than I."

"I'm sorry. I don't know what you're talking about."

"You are new indeed on Kropotkin," the old man said. "Just a moment." He went into his house and emerged with a small power pack. He indicated it to Ronny Bronston. "This is our destruction," he said.

The Section G agent shook his head, bewildered.

The old-timer sat down again. "My son," he said, "runs the farm now. Six months ago, he traded one of our colts for a small pump, powered by one of these. It was little use on my part to argue against the step. The pump eliminates considerable work at the well and in irrigation."

Ronny still didn't understand.

"The power pack is dead now," the old man said, "and my son needs a new one."

"They're extremely cheap," Ronny said. "An industrialized planet turns them out in multi-million amounts at practically no cost."

"We have little with which to trade. A few handicrafts, at most."

Ronny said, "But, good heavens, man, build yourselves a plant to manufacture power packs. With a population this small, a factory employing no more than half a dozen men could turn out all you need."

The old man was shaking his head. He held up the battery. "This comes from the planet Archimedes," he said, "one of the most highly industrialized in the UP, so I understand. On Archimedes do you know how many persons it takes to manufacture this power pack?"

"A handful to operate the whole factory. Archimedes is fully automated."

The old man was still moving his head negatively. "No. It takes the total working population of the planet. How many different metals do you think are contained in it, in all? I can immediately see what must be lead and copper."

Ronny said uncomfortably, "Probably at least a dozen, some microscopic amounts."

"That's right. So we need a highly developed metallurgical industry before we can even begin. Then a developed transportation industry to take metals to the factory. We need

71

power to run the factory, hydro-electric, solar or possibly atomic power. We need a tool-making industry to equip the factory, the transport industry and the power industry. And while the men are employed in these, we need farmers to produce food for them, educators to teach them the sciences and techniques involved, and an entertainment industry to amuse them in their hours of rest. As their lives become more complicated with all this, we need a developed medical industry to keep them in health."

The old man hesitated for a moment, then said, "And, above all, we need a highly complicated government to keep all this accumulation of wealth in check and balance. No. You see, my friend, it takes *social labor* to produce products such as this, and thus far we have avoided that on Kropotkin. In fact, it was for such avoidance that my ancestors originally came to this planet."

Ronny said, scowling, "This gets ridiculous. You show me this basically simple power pack and say it will ruin your socio-economic system. On the face of it, it's ridiculous."

The old man sighed and looked out over the village unseeingly. "It's not just that single item, of course. The other day one of my neighbors turned up with a light bulb with built-in power for a year's time. It is the envy of the unthinking persons of the neighborhood, most of whom would give a great deal for such a source of light. A nephew of mine has somehow even acquired a powered bicycle, I think you call them, from somewhere or other. One by one, item by item, these products of advanced technology turn up— from whence, we don't seem to be able to find out."

Under his breath, Ronny muttered, *"Paine"*.

"I beg your pardon?" the old man said.

"Nothing," the Section G agent said. He leaned forward and, a worried frown working its way over his face, began to question the other more closely.

XIII

AFTERWARD, Ronny Bronston strode slowly toward the UP headquarters. There was only a small contingent of United Planets personnel on this little-populated member planet but, as always, there seemed to be an office for Section G.

Ronny stood outside it for a moment. There were voices from within, but he didn't knock.

In fact, he cast his eyes up and down the short corridor. At the far end was a desk with a girl in the Interplanetary Cultural Exchange Department working away in concentration. She wasn't looking in his direction.

Ronny Bronston put his ear to the door. The building was primitive enough in its construction to permit his hearing.

Tog Lee Chang Chu was saying seriously, "Oh, it was chaotic all right, but no, I don't really believe it could have been a Tommy Paine case. Actually I'd suggest to you that you run over to Catalina. When I was on Avalon I heard rumors that Tommy Paine's finger seemed to be stirring around in the mess there. Yes, I'd recommend that you take off for Catalina immediately. If Paine is anywhere in this vicinity at all, it would be Catalina."

For a moment, Ronny Bronston froze. Then in automatic reflex his hand went inside his jacket to rest over the butt of the Model H automatic there.

No, that wasn't the answer. His hand dropped away from the gun.

He listened further.

Another voice was saying, "We thought we were on the trail for awhile on Hector, but it turned out it wasn't Paine. Just a group of local agitators fed up with the communist regime there. There's going to be a blood bath on Hector before they're through, but it doesn't seem to be Paine's work this time."

Tog's voice was musing. "Well, you never know; it sounds like the sort of muck he likes to play in."

The strange voice said argumentatively, "Well, Hector *needs* a few fundamental changes."

"It could be," Tog said, "but that's their internal affairs, of course. Our job in Section G is to prevent troubles between the differing socio-economic and religious features of member planets. Whatever we think of some of the things Paine does, our task is to get him."

Ronny Bronston pushed the door open and went through. Tog Lee Chang Chu was sitting at a desk, nonchalant and petitely beautiful as usual; comfortably seated in easy-chairs were two young men whose attire suggested they were probably citizens of United Planets and possibly even Earthlings.

"Hello, Ronny," Tog said softly. "Meet Frederic Lippman and Pedro Nazaré, both Section G operatives. This is my colleague, Ronald Bronston, gentlemen. Frederic and Pedro were just leaving, Ronny."

The two agents got up to shake hands.

Ronny said, "You can't be in that much of a hurry. What's your assignment, boys?"

Lippmen, an earnest type, and by his appearance not more than twenty-five or so years of age, began to answer, but Nazaré said hurriedly, "Actually, it's a confidential assignment. We're working directly out of the Octagon."

Lippman said, frowning, "It's not *that* confidential, Tog. Bronston's an agent, too. What's your assignment, Ronny?"

Ronny said very slowly, "I'm beginning to suspect that it's the same as yours, and various other pieces are beginning to fall into place."

Lippman was taken aback. "You mean you're looking for Tommy Paine?" His eyes went to his associate. "How could that be, Tog? I didn't know more than one of us were on this job. Why, that means if Bronston here finds him first, I won't get my permanent appointment."

Ronny looked at Tog Lee Chang Chu, who was sitting demurely, hands in lap, a resigned expression on her face. He said, "And if you find him first, I won't get mine. Look here, Tog, how many men does Sid Jakes have out on this assignment?"

"I wouldn't know," she said mildly.

He snapped. "A few dozen or so? Or possibly a few hundred?"

"It seems unlikely there could be that many," she said mildly. She looked at the other two agents. "I think you two had better run along. Take my suggestion I made earlier."

"Wait a minute," Ronny snapped. "You mean that they go to Catalina? That's ridiculous."

Tog Lee Chang Chu looked at Pedro Nazaré and he turned and started for the door, followed by Frederic Lippman, who was still scowling his puzzlement.

"Wait a minute!" Ronny snapped. "I tell you it's ridiculous. And why follow her suggestions? She's just my assistant."

Pedro Nazaré said, "Come on, Fred, let's get going, we'll have to pack." But Lippman wasn't having any.

"His assistant?" he said to Tog Lee Chang Chu.

Tog Lee Chang Chu's face changed expression in sudden decision. She opened her bag and brought forth a Section G identification wallet and flicked it open. The badge was gold. "I suggest you hurry," she said to the two agents.

They left, and Tog turned back to Ronny, her eyebrows raised questioningly.

Ronny sank down into one of the chairs recently occupied by the other two agents and tried to unravel thoughts. He said finally, "I suppose my question should be, why do Ross Metaxa and Sid Jakes send an agent of supervisor rank to act as assistant to a probationary agent? But that's not what I'm asking yet. First, Lippman just called his buddy Tog. How come?"

Tog took her seat again, rueful resignation on her face. "You should be figuring it out on your own by this time, Ronny."

He looked at her belligerently. "I'm too stupid, eh?" The anger was growing within him.

"Tog," she said. "It's a nickname, or possibly you might call it a title. Tog. T-O-G. The Other Guy. My name is Lee Chang Chu, and I'm of supervisor grade presently working

75

at developing new Section G operatives. Considering the continuing rapid growth of UP, and the continuing crises that come up in UP activities, developing new operatives is one of the department's most pressing jobs. Each new agent, on his first assignment, is always paired with an experienced old-timer."

"I see," he said flatly. "Your principal job being to needle the fledgling, eh?"

She lowered her eyes. "I wouldn't exactly word it that way," she said. She was obviously unrepentant.

He said, "You must get a lot of laughs out of it. If I say it seems to me democracy is a good thing, you give me an argument about the superiority of rule by an elite. If I say anarchism is ridiculous, you dredge up an opinion that it's man's highest ethic. You must laugh yourself to sleep at nights. You and Metaxa and Jakes and every other agent in Section G. Everybody is in on the Tog gag but the sucker."

"Sometimes there are amusing elements to the work," Lee Chang conceded, demurely.

"Just one more thing I'd like to ask," Ronny rapped. "This first assignment agents are given. Is it always to look for Tommy Paine?"

She looked up at him, said nothing, but her eyes were questioning.

"Don't worry," he snapped. "I've already found out who Paine is."

"Ah?" She was suddenly interested. "Then I'm glad I ordered that other probationary agent to leave. Evidently he hasn't. Obviously I didn't want the two of you comparing notes."

"No, that would never do," he said bitterly. "Well, this is the end of the assignment so far as you and I are concerned. I'm heading back for Earth."

"Of course," she said.

XIV

HE HAD TIME on the way to think it all over, and over and over again, and a great deal of it simply didn't make sense. He had enough information to be disillusioned, sick at heart. A lifetime? At least three. His father and his grandfather before him had had the dream. He'd been weaned on the idealistic purposes of the United Planets and man's fated growth into the stars.

He was a third-generation dreamer of participating in the glory. His grandfather had been a citizen of Earth and had given up a commercial position to take a job that amounted to little more than a janitor in an obscure department of Interplanetary Financial Clearing. He'd wanted to get into the big job, into space, but had never made it. Ronny's father had managed to work up to the point where he was a supervisor in Interplanetary Medical Exchange, in the tabulating department. He too had wanted into space, and had never made it. Ronny had loved them both. In a way, fulfilling his own dreams had been a debt he owed them, because at the same time he was fulfilling theirs.

And now this. All that had been gold was suddenly gilted lead. The dream had become contemptuous nightmare.

Finally back in Greater Washington, he went immediately from the shuttleport to the Octagon. His Bureau of Investigation badge was enough to see him through the guide-guards and all the way through to the office of Irene Kasansky.

She looked up at him quickly. "Hi," she said. "Ronny Bronston, isn't it?"

"That's right. I want to see Commissioner Metaxa."

She scowled. "I can't work you in now. How about Sid Jakes?"

He said, "Jakes is in charge of the Tommy Paine routine, isn't he?"

77

She shot a sharper look up at him. "That's right," she said warily.

"All right," Ronny said. "I'll see Jakes."

Her deft right hand slipped open a drawer in her desk. "You'd better leave your gun here," she said. "I've known probationary agents to get excited, in my time."

He looked at her.

And she looked back, her gaze level.

Ronny Bronston shrugged, slipped the Model H from under his armpit and tossed it into the drawer.

Irene Kasansky went back to her work. "You know the way," she said.

This time Ronny Bronston pushed open the door to Sid Jakes' office without knocking. The Section G supervisor was poring over reports on his desk. He looked up and grinned his Sid Jakes grin.

"Ronny!" he said. "Welcome back. You know, you're one of the quickest men ever to return from a Tommy Paine assignment. I was talking to Lee Chang only a day or so ago. She said you were on your way."

Ronny grunted, his anger growing within him. He lowered himself into one of the room's heavy chairs, and glared at the other.

Sid Jakes chuckled and leaned back in his chair. "Before we go any further, just to check, who is Tommy Paine?"

Ronny snapped, "You are."

The supervisor's eyebrows went up.

Ronny said, "You and Ross Metaxa and Lee Chang Chu—and all the rest of Section G. Section G is Tommy Paine."

"Good man!" Sid Jakes chortled. He flicked a switch on his order box. "Irene," he said, "how about clearing me through to the commissioner? I want to take Ronny in for his finals."

Irene snapped back something and Sid Jakes switched off and turned to Ronny happily. "Let's go," he said. "Ross is free for a time."

Ronny Bronston said nothing. He followed the other. The rage within him was still mounting.

In the months that had elapsed since Ronny Bronston had seen Ross Metaxa the latter had changed not at all. His clothing was still sloppy, his eyes bleary with lack of sleep or abundance of alcohol—or both. His expression was still sour and skeptical.

He looked up at their entry and scowled, and made no effort to rise and shake hands. He said to Ronny sourly, "O.K., sound off and get it over with. I haven't too much time this afternoon."

Ronny Bronston was just beginning to feel tentacles of cold doubt, but he suppressed them. The boiling anger was uppermost. He said flatly, "All my life I've been a dedicated United Planets man. All my life I've considered its efforts the most praiseworthy and greatest endeavor man has ever attempted."

"Of course, old chap," Jakes told him cheerfully. "We know all that, or you wouldn't ever have been chosen as an agent for Section G."

Ronny looked at him in disgust. "I've resigned that position, Jakes."

Jakes grinned back at him. "To the contrary, you're now in the process of receiving permanent appointment."

Ronny snorted his disgust and turned back to Metaxa. "Section G is a secret department of the Bureau of Investigation devoted to subverting Article One of the United Planets Charter."

Metaxa nodded.

"You don't deny it?"

Metaxa shook his head.

"Article One," Ronny snapped, "is the basic foundation of the Charter which every member of UP and particularly every citizen of United Planets, such as ourselves, has sworn to uphold. But the very reason for the existence of this Section G is to interfere with the internal affairs of member planets, to subvert their governments, their economic systems, their religions, their ideals, their very ways of life."

Metaxa yawned and reached into a desk drawer for his bottle. "That's right," he said. "Anybody like a drink?"

Ronny ignored him. "I'm surprised I didn't catch on even sooner," he said. "On New Delos Mouley Hassan, the local agent, knew the God-King was going to be assassinated. He brought in extra agents and even a detail of Space Forces guards for the emergency. He probably engineered the assassination himself."

"Nope," Jakes said. "We seldom go *that* far. Local rebels did the actual work, but, admittedly, we knew what they were planning. In fact, I've got a sneaking suspicion that Mouley Hassan provided them with the bomb. That lad's a bit too dedicated."

"But *why?*" Ronny blurted. "That's deliberately interfering with internal affairs. If the word got out, every planet in UP would resign."

"Probably no planet in the system that needed a change so badly," Metaxa growled. "If they were ever going to swing into real progress, that hierarchy of priests had to go." He snorted. "An immortal God-King, yet."

Ronny pressed on. "That was bad enough, but how about this planet Mother, where the colonists had attempted to return and live in the manner man did in earliest times."

"Most backward planet in the UP," Metaxa said sourly. "They just had to be roused."

"And Kropotkin!" Ronny blurted. "Don't you understand, those people were happy there. Their lives were simple, uncomplicated, and they had achieved a happiness that—"

Metaxa came to his feet. He scowled at Ronny Bronston and growled, "Unfortunately, the human race can't take the time out for happiness. Come along. I want to show you something."

He swung around the corner of his desk and made his way toward a ceiling-high bookcase.

Ronny stared after him, taken off guard, but Sid Jakes was grinning his amusement.

Ross Metaxa pushed a concealed button and the bookcase slid away to one side to reveal an elevator beyond.

"Come along," Metaxa repeated over his shoulder. He entered the elevator, followed by Jakes.

PLANETARY AGENT X

There was nothing else to do. Ronny Bronston followed them, his face still flushed with the angered argument.

The elevator dropped—how far, Ronny had no idea. It stopped and they emerged into a plain, sparsely furnished vault. Against one wall was a boxlike affair that reminded Ronny of nothing so much as a deep-freeze.

For all practical purposes, that's what it was. Ross Metaxa led him over and they stared down into its glass-covered interior.

Ronny's eyes bugged. The box contained the partly charred body of an animal approximately the size of a rabbit. No, not an animal. It had obviously once been clothed, and its limbs were obviously those of a tool-using life form.

Metaxa and Jakes were staring down at it solemnly, for once no inane grin on the supervisor's face. And that of Ross Metaxa was more weary than ever.

Ronny said finally, "What is it?" But he knew.

"You tell us," Metaxa growled sourly.

"It's an intelligent life form," Ronny blurted. "Why has it been kept secret?"

"Let's go back upstairs," Metaxa sighed.

Back in his office he said, "Now I go into my speech. Shut up for awhile." He poured himself a drink, not offering one to the other two. "Ronny," he said, "man isn't alone in the galaxy. There's other intelligent life. Dangerously intelligent."

In spite of himself Ronny reacted in amusement. "That little creature down there? The size of a small monkey?" As soon as he said it, he realized the ridiculousness of his statement.

Metaxa grunted. "Obviously size means nothing. That little fellow down there was picked up by one of our Space Forces scouts over a century ago. How long he'd been drifting through space, we don't know. Possibly only months, but possibly hundreds of centuries. But however long, he's proof that man is not alone in the galaxy. And we have no way of knowing when the expanding human race will come up against this other intelligence—and whoever it was fighting."

"But," Ronny protested, "you're assuming they're aggressive. Perhaps coming in contact with these aliens will be the best thing that ever happened to man. Possibly that little fellow down there is the most benevolent creature ever evolved."

Metaxa looked at him strangely. "Let's hope so," he said. "However, when found he was in what must have been a one-man scout. He was dead and his craft was blasted and torn—obviously from some sort of weapons' fire. His scout was obviously a military craft, highly equipped with what could only be weapons, most of them so damaged our engineers haven't been able to figure them out. To the extent they have been able to reconstruct them, they're scared silly. No, there's no two ways about it, our little rabbit sized intelligence down in the vault was killed in an interplanetary conflict. And sooner or later, Ronny, man in his explosion into the stars is going to run into either or both of the opponents in that conflict."

Ronny Bronston slumped back into his chair, his brain running out a dozen leads at once.

Metaxa and Jakes remained quiet, looking at him speculatively.

Ronny said slowly, "Then the purpose of Section G is to push the member planets of UP along the fastest path of progress, to get them ready for the eventual meeting."

"Not just Section G," Metaxa growled, "but all of the United Planets organization, although most of the rank and file don't even know our basic purpose. Section G? We do the dirty work, and are proud to do it, by every method we can devise."

Ronny leaned forward. "But look," he said. "Why not simply inform all member planets of this common danger? They'd all unite in the effort to meet the common potential foe. Anything standing in the way would be brushed aside."

Metaxa shook his head wearily. "Would they? Is a common danger enough for man to change his institutions, particularly those pertaining to property, power and religion? History doesn't show it. Delve back into early times and you'll recall, for an example, that in man's early discovery of nuclear weapons he almost destroyed himself. Three or four different socio-economic systems coexisted at that time and all would have preferred destruction rather than changes in their social forms."

Jakes said, in an unwonted quiet tone, "No, until someone comes up with a better answer it looks as though Section G is going to have to continue the job of advancing man's institutions, in spite of himself."

The commissioner made it clearer. "It's not as though we deal with all our member planets. It isn't necessary. But you see, Ronny, the best colonists are usually made up of the, well, crackpot element. Those who are satisfied stay at home. America, for instance, was settled by the adventurers, the malcontents, the nonconformists, the religious cultists, and even the fugitives and criminals of Europe. So it is in the stars. A group of colonists go out with their dreams, their schemes, their far-out ideas. In a few centuries they've populated their new planet, and often do very well indeed. But often not and a nudge, a push, from Section G can start them up another rung or so of the ladder of social evolution. Most of them don't want the push. Few cultures, if any, realize they are mortal; like Hitler's Reich, they expect to last at least a thousand years. They resist any change—even change for the better."

Ronny's defenses were crumbling, but he threw one last punch. "How do you know the changes you make are for the better?"

Metaxa shrugged heavy shoulders. "It's sometimes difficult to decide, but we aim for changes that will mean an increased scientific progress, a more advanced industrial technology, more and better education, the opening of opportunity for every member of the culture to exert himself to the full of his abilities. The last is particularly important. Too many cultures, even those that think of themselves as particularly advanced, suppress the individual by one means or another."

Ronny was still mentally reeling with the magnitude of it all. "But how can you account for the fact that these alien intelligences haven't already come in contact with us?"

Metaxa shrugged again. "The Solar System, our sun, is way out in a sparsely populated spiral arm of our galaxy. Undoubtedly these others are further in toward the center. We have no way of knowing how far away they are, or how many sun systems they dominate, or even how *many* other empires of intelligent life forms there are. All we know is that there are other intelligences in the galaxy, that they are near enough like us to live on the same type planets. The more opportunity man has to develop before the initial contact takes place, the stronger bargaining position, or military position, as the case may be, he'll be in."

Sid Jakes summed up the Tommy Paine business for Ronny's sake. "We need capable agents badly, but we need dedicated and efficient ones. We can't afford anything less. So when we come upon potential Section G operatives we send them out with a trusted Tog to get a picture of these United Planets of ours. It's the quickest method of indoctrination we've hit upon; the agent literally teaches himself by observation and participation. Usually, it takes four or five stops, on this planet and that, before the probationary agent begins sympathizing with the efforts of this elusive Tommy Paine. Especially since every Section G agent he runs into, including the Tog, of course, fills him full of stories of Tommy Paine's activities.

"You were one of the quickest to stumble on the true nature of our Section G. After calling at only three planets you saw that we ourselves are Tommy Paine."

"But . . . but what's the end?" Ronny said plaintively. "You say our job is advancing man, even in spite of himself when it comes to that. We start at the bottom of the evolutionary ladder in a condition of savagery, clan communism in government, simple animism in religion, and slowly we progress through barbarism to civilization, through paganism to the higher ethical codes, through chattel slavery and then feudalism and beyond. What is the final end, the Ultima Thule?"

Metaxa was shaking his head again. He poured himself another drink, offered the bottle this time to the others. "We don't know," he said wearily. "Perhaps there is none. Perhaps there is always another rung on this evolutionary ladder." He punched at his order box and said, "Irene, have them do up a silver badge for Ronny."

Ronny Bronston took a deep breath and reached for the brown bottle. "Well," he said, "I suppose I'm ready to ask for my first assignment."

It was Sid Jakes who looked at him glumly. "You're not going to like it, you know."

Ronny poured the drink. "How do you mean?" But in a way, he knew what the other meant.

Sid said, "We're all the same in Section G, Ronny. We come in all Gung Ho. We're burning with romantic enthusiasm. No other types are encouraged in this agency—can't be. And what do we find? We find ourselves in the Department of Dirty Tricks. Half our work comes under the head of Machiavellianism. Oh, sure, your first assignment might be above-board routine. And maybe even your second. But sooner or later you'll run into one of the jobs for which we *really* exist. One of the jobs where it's up to you to sacrifice an. individual, a city, sometimes even a whole nation, for the sake of the long range view of United Planets. That's when the guts of your conscience are strained, Ronny."

Metaxa growled, "What're you trying to do, run him away?"

Sid grunted a caricature of his usual humor. "There's no running him away. Ronny's slated to be as dedicated a Section G operative as we've ever had. I was just wondering how we're going to feel when he pulls off his first *real* assignment. And just wondering how he's going to feel about himself."

Then he too reached for the tequila bottle.

PLANETARY AGENT X

PART TWO

XV

BILLY ANTRIM WAS riding hard. He had little sure knowledge of just how far behind him the sheriff's men might be—nor, for that matter, of how many they were.

He was keeping off the roads as much as he could, but that was becoming increasingly difficult since the area was far from sparsely populated now that he was approaching the city. His only chance, he figured, was to get to the city and go to ground.

He twisted and turned over the open fields, trying to keep to such cover as was offered by clumps of trees, by gullies, by lines of fence. And from time to time he cast a glance over his shoulder.

Not that Billy was particularly afraid. Scared, he would have called it. In his profession, you couldn't afford that emotion. A pistolero in action is cool—he either keeps that way, under stress, or he doesn't long survive. And thus far Billy Antrim had survived—in spades.

He rode hard and he rode deviously, and from time to time unconsciously he loosened the gun wedged into his belt. For in spite of manufacturers of quick-draw holsters to the contrary, the fastest draw is from the belt.

He could see the lights of the city ahead. In fact, he had been able to see them for some time. He became more optimistic. His favorite slogan was, *one chance in a million*, but he felt he had better than that now. At least so far as getting to the city was concerned. Beyond that . . .

It was then that he picked up the sound behind him. His ears were good, with the sensitiveness of the organs of youth, since Billy Antrim was nineteen years of age. There was no doubt in his mind. At this time of night, others would have been sticking to the roads, not riding madly over fields, crossing streams, thundering up and down hillocks.

PLANETARY AGENT X

He darted a look back. Spotted them. Shot a calculating glance toward the city ahead. He would never make it. They were coming up fast. How many of them, he still didn't know.

"One chance in a million," Billy muttered. He sneered his own brand of amusement.

He was a slight youth, just past the pimply age, with a sallow face, dirty blond hair and baby-blue eyes—the traditional eyes of the man killer. His teeth were buckteeth enough usually to show through his lips. In spite of youth, he could never have been called good looking. He was five foot eight, weighed slightly less than one fifty, and he moved with the grace of a girl—no, not a girl; with the grace of a panther on the hunt.

There was an outcropping of rocks immediately before him, out of place in this vicinity of gentle fields. He quickly swung around it and came to a halt. His hope was that their eyes were as keen as his own and that they had already spotted him and knew that they were closing in. The other man's reflexes weren't usually as fast as those of Billy Antrim's and now that was all he had left to depend upon.

When they came slewing around the rock outcropping, slowed a bit in view of the fact that they couldn't be sure exactly where he had gone beyond, Billy was standing there, at comfortable ease, the short barreled gun in his hand and already half aimed.

There were two of them. Only two.

He had flicked the selector switch to full blast, automatic. Now he gently squeezed the trigger and the windshield of the pursuing floater shattered into slivers and dust and the vehicle, suddenly driverless, banked to the left, crashing into the rock pile in a grinding, collapsing, shrieking complaint of agonized machinery, framework and glass.

He stood for a moment, the gun still at the ready, though there was small chance that any life could have survived his attack. He watched expressionlessly, poker-faced, feeling nothing whatsoever in the way of regret or compassion. They had played the game of pursuit and lost. What was there to

87

regret, so far as he was concerned? He had won, in his one chance in a million gamble.

He tucked the gun back into his belt and scrambled to the top of the rocks, marveling as he went that there should be comparatively open countryside this near to Greater Washington. It was deliberate, undoubtedly. Evidently the largest city on Earth had some desperate need of a bit of countryside surrounding it. What amounted to a national park, where there were air, trees, and even an occasional stream. A memory of what the world had been in yesteryear.

From the top he surveyed back over the route he had just covered. So far as he could see, there were no further pursuers. They had evidently sent no more than two men, confident that with radar, sensi-screens and their other ultramodern police equipment and armament, one man posed no problems. There was the faintest of smiles on his usually poker-face.

He returned to his floater, lifted it and headed toward the city. He would have to plan carefully now. Undoubtedly his two pursuers had been in continual communications with their headquarters. Suddenly their reports would have been cut off. Headquarters would undoubtedly send out more men, but, what was more pressing, would call ahead for the city's police to be on the watch for him. .

Billy Antrim's problems were far from over.

Ronald Bronston said to Irene, "What's roiling the Old Man?"

She paused long enough from her switches, her order-box, her buttons and phones to say snappishly, "How would I know? He never tells me what's going on around here. I'm supposed to be clairvoyant, telepathic, and omniscient to boot. I tell you, there's a lot of jetsam around this office."

Ronny grinned at her. "Sid Jakes called and said Ross wanted to see me immediately."

Irene Kasansky was as important a cog in the wheels of Section G, of the Bureau of Investigation, of the Department of Justice, of the Commissariat of Interplanetary Affairs, of

United Planets, as was Ross Metaxa himself. Or so, at least, everybody said, including the Old Man when he was slightly in his cups. She loved every soul in the small department and the affection was reciprocated with interest—though no one would have dreamed of admitting it, on either side.

She said now, "Well, don't stand there. If his high mucky-muck summoned you, scamper." She added, "Tell him he can have up to fifteen minutes with you. Then he's got to see Lee Chang about the Han rebellion."

"Got it," Ronny told her, making for the inner door.

She looked after him for a split second, deciding that of all the top field agents in Section G, Ronny Bronston least looked the part, which was possibly to be one of his most valuable assets. Irene loved them all, these spearhead men of the conquest of space, but there was a particular something about Ronny Bronston. She snorted inwardly—first thing she knew she'd be letting him catch onto the fact, and then where would things be?

Ronny went through the entry and turned left to the door inconspicuously lettered, ROSS METAXA, COMMISSIONER, SECTION G.

Section G, Ronny thought, all over again. *What an innocuous name for Department of Trouble-shooting, Department of Cloak and Dagger, Department of Secret Treasury. Department devoted*, he reminded himself bitterly, *to the principle that the end justifies the means.* Ronny had yet to forget he had been raised in an atmosphere of high ethic and ideals.

Ronny knocked and the door slid open.

Ross Metaxa, bleary eyed as always, looked up, as always affecting the acid surliness which fooled everybody—sometimes even himself.

He pushed some reports away from that part of his desk immediately before him and fished the brown bottle from a drawer as he said, "Sit down, Ronny. Drink?"

"Not from that bottle," Ronny said.

"How's the wound?" Metaxa growled, pouring himself a slug. "Doctor got you off booze?"

"I'm okay now. I've got *myself* off that Denebian tequila of yours," Ronny said, sinking into a chair. "I know when I'm well off. I'll stick to kerosene."

"Very funny," Metaxa grumbled, knocking the liquor back over his tonsils, impervious to the other's shudder. He put the top back on the bottle, began to return it to the drawer, changed his mind and shoved it to one side of the desk. "What do you know about Palermo?" he said.

Ronny cast his eyes slightly upward and spoke as though remembering a lesson. "One of the far out planets, in more ways than space. Colonized by Italians . . ."

"Sicilians," Metaxa grunted.

". . . only recently joining the UP. The government and socio-economic system seem to be unique."

His superior grunted sour amusement. "That's a gentle way of putting it," he said. "The government is by *Maffeo,* a very old Sicilian institution which they seem to export along with their emigrants. Its origins are lost in antiquity but seem to go as far back as the slave rebellions of the Romans."

"Romans?"

"What's wrong with your history, Ronny?" the other said gruffly. "The Roman Empire. Controlled . . ."

"Oh, yeah. I remember."

The other grunted. "You can look it up in the archives later. At any rate, it seems that the planet Palermo was originally settled by peasant types, evidently largely interested in fleeing this very institution. They found their planet, way beyond what were then the reaches of UP, and paid through the nose to have themselves and their scanty belongings hauled out. Space Freightways handled the transportation. One of their usual gyp arrangements."

Metaxa came to a sudden halt in his delivery and said into his order-box, "Irene, what ever happened to that investigation on Space Freightways? I told you I wanted an immediate report."

Ronny Bronston couldn't make out her answer, but he caught the snap in her voice. He grinned inwardly.

"All right, all right," Metaxa snapped back. "But tell that

loafer to get a move on." He grunted and turned back to Ronny.

"At any rate, the colonists of Palermo managed to foul up their whole project through sheer lack of sophistication. Planted in their number were a handful of the very Maffeo they thought they were getting away from. In less than two generations, the outfit was in control."

"In what way?" Ronny said.

"In the most brutal way," Metaxa told him sourly. "You can look up details later. What interests us is that at this time the planet is stagnating under what amounts to a modern form of robber baron feudalism. A handful of bully-boys on the top, a terrified peasantry working their lives away on the bottom."

"They're members of UP?" Ronny said. "Why'd we let them in? As long as they were outside, we could have dealt with them. A few agents could have drifted in and pulled some . . ."

Metaxa was nodding. "Because we were stupid, and they were smart, instinctively smart. Luigi Agrigento, current head of the Maffeo, saw the handwriting on the wall when nearby planets began also to be colonized. He petitioned to join UP and was admitted after the usual mild routine. He understood perfectly well that given membership, Articles One and Two of the United Planets Charter protected him from outside interference.

"And if he'd left it at that, he probably would have gotten away indefinitely with his usurpation of power on Palermo. But that wasn't the Maffeo way, and never has been. Last year, one of his victims, named Giorgio Schiavoni, managed to stow away on an Avalon trader which had stopped off at Palermo, and after various difficulties wrangled his way here to Earth, where he presented himself at the Commissariat of Interplanetary Affairs and told a rather bloodcurdling tale of suppression on his home planet. He claimed to represent a majority of the planet's population and requested aid. The Palermo Embassy, of course, put up a howl, invoking Article One."

91

Ronny said harshly, "Some of our member planets *need* interfering with."

Ross Metaxa glowered at him, took up his bottle and poured himself another jolt. "Bronston, if you ever express that opinion publicly, you're out. You're out so fast, and so hard, you'll never get a place in UP again, not to speak of this department. Don't ever forget, Ronald Bronston, that the job of Section G is to advance member planets in their socio-economic systems, their political systems, on certain occasions in their religious systems—but that if we let that fact out, we're sunk. Needless to say, Palermo is one of the worlds that would prefer to stay just as it is, threat from aliens or no threat. At least, that's the way Luigi Agrigento and his Maffeo see it. The majority of the peasantry would have other views."

"And that's where this Giorgio Schiavoni comes in, eh?"

Metaxa's heavy face worked. "That's where he used to come in. Schiavoni did the unforgiveable, given the Maffeo philosophy. He talked. Yesterday, he was shot down leaving the apartment we had assigned him over in the Pittsburg area."

Ronny stared at him. "Shot down! You mean a man was *assassinated* right here on Earth?"

"Exactly. Luigi Agrigento's hand was evidently long enough to stretch all the way from Palermo. It gives you some idea of his methods."

Ronny was flabbergasted.

Metaxa wrapped it up. "Your job is the only angle we've come up with, so far. It's to track down and either, preferably, capture or if necessary liquidate the professional killer who did the job."

"He *escaped?*"

Metaxa said grimly. "Thus far. I'm rushed now, Ronny. Sid Jakes will give you more details, physical description and so forth." His face went hard. "But I'll finish up with this: Giorgio Schiavoni's death will be atoned for. He threw himself on the mercy of United Planets, in a patriot's cause, and his protection was left in the hands of this department. There hasn't been a political assassination on Earth in the memory of anyone living and we allowed ourselves to be careless. Very well, but Schiavoni will be vindicated, that I promise."

Ronny came to his feet. "I'll see Jakes," he said simply.

The office door of Ross Metaxa's right hand man was, as always, slightly ajar.

When Ronny knocked, Sid's voice yelled out happily, "Come on in! It's always open!"

Ronny braced himself and entered. He was still not quite used to the Sid Jakes personality.

The supervisor was as informal in appearance as his boss, if not more so. Ronny sometimes wondered how either of them ever got past the Octagon guards when coming to work in the morning. Jakes invariably looked more like a man in his oldest sports clothes taking off on a weekend fishing, rather than a high ranking official in the staid Octagon.

"Ronny!" he exclaimed, bouncing up from his chair and speeding around the corner of his desk. "Thought you were in the hospital!"

He wrapped his arms around the other and chortled happily. "I told you, when you're dodging bullets, you ought to zig instead of zagging."

Ronny had to laugh at him. "And vice versa?" he said.

"As the occasion calls. Sit down, sit down. I read the reports on your assignment on Goshen. Pulled off a neat trick there."

"Yeah," Ronny grunted. "And wound up with a hole in my side."

Sid Jakes zipped around to the other side of his desk again and into his chair. "And got a three month vacation," he pointed out. "You field men get all the breaks."

"Yeah," Ronny said.

Sid Jakes turned serious for a brief moment, the longest known period for him. He said, "I see you're on this Billy Antrim job."

"Billy Antrim?"

"This assassin from Palermo."

Ronny said, "The Old Man didn't give me his name. You were to fill in the details."

The Section G supervisor popped his feet up onto the desk. "Okay. Here they come. The lad you're chasing is named Billy Antrim. Not William, Billy. Our dossier on him isn't complete as yet. And maybe it'll never be completed, if you're able to pull off your assignment quickly."

Ronny said, "I don't see how he could have remained uncaught even this long."

"Because he's a cunning snake," Sid told him, grinning as though that made the whole thing happier. "He's a lad who's never done anything in his adult life except use a gun. If you can call him an adult."

Ronny looked at him quizzically.

Sid Jakes took up a report from a desk almost as littered as that of Ross Metaxa. He puckered his lips. "He's not twenty yet, according to this. At any rate, here's the rundown. Our Billy wasn't born on Palermo; he came there as a child with his mother. She was evidently some sort of entertainer, probably on a rather low level. To cut things short, one of Luigi Agrigento's bully boys evidently gave her a hard time one night. Cuffed her around a bit, for playing too hard to get. And our Billy, who was eleven or twelve at the time, knifed the man to death." Sid chortled. "Mind you, this chap was one of Luigi's bodyguards. And a twelve-year-old finished him off. Neat trick, eh?"

"Very neat," Ronny said dryly.

Sid Jakes chuckled. "Now you'd think that would get friend Luigi all riled up, but not at all. He evidently thought it was the funniest thing that had happened since his grandmother fell down the well. He had Ruth Antrim, the mother, kicked off the planet—for her own protection, since they've got vendetta traditions on Palermo that evidently apply even to women—but took over the care of the boy himself."

"I can see what's coming," Ronny said.

"Right. The boy was a crack shot before he was fifteen. Which was just as well, since he killed his second man at that age. Some relative of his first victim who evidently de-

94

cided vengeance was in order even though Billy was under
Agrigento's protection. He had evidently also learned to
throw a knife and . . ."

"Throw a knife?" Ronny said blankly.

"That's right. Evidently they've got some skills preserved
on Palermo that have died off elsewhere," Sid said happily.
"But you might remember that knife routine. And Billy's
not on the large side, even smaller than you, but evidently
he can use his knife doing close-in work too." Sid Jakes
grinned. "You beginning to love him more and more?"

"More and more," Ronny said.

"It seems that Luigi was pleased as Punch with his protégé and began to use him as a professional pistolero. Government on Palermo, it appears, doesn't call for courts of law,
judges, juries, jails and that sort of jetsam." Sid beamed.
"Not at all. The Maffeo takes care of all those little things. At
any rate, our charming Billy became quite adept at his trade.
A real pro. So much so that when Luigi got in a tizzy about
Giorgio Schiavoni escaping from Palermo, and above all
sounding off to the Commissariat of Interplanetary Affairs, he
sent Billy Antrim to set things right."

Ronny said, "How did he ever expect Antrim to make his
getaway?"

Sid Jakes took his heels from the desk and leaned forward,
beaming. He pointed a finger at Ronny. "Now that's the real
beauty of the thing. Our Luigi knew damn well that young
Billy wouldn't ever succeed in making a getaway and hence
made no effort to provide one."

Ronny frowned. "You mean Antrim knew he'd get caught,
but pulled the job anyway?"

Sid shook his head. "Not if our dope is correct. Luigi Agrigento figured on throwing Billy to the wolves. He let the boy
believe there was a getaway all arranged. But there simply
wasn't."

The field man didn't get it. "But I thought Antrim was his
favorite protégé. He wouldn't . . ."

Sid Jakes chuckled. "I keep telling you about these Maffeo
lads. They're very uncouth, as the term goes. Luigi isn't the

95

type to let friendship, or affection, interfere with business and there was one advantage in sending Billy to do the job. Billy isn't a citizen of Palermo, having been born on Delos. When blame is being scattered around, Agrigento will have some claim to innocence."

Ronny whistled softly. "Well, what happened here on Earth?"

"It was done very professionally indeed. A classical assassination of the very old school, such as you see in the historical Tri-D shows. Giorgio Schiavoni, was located, set up, and fingered. And Billy shot him very neatly indeed, like the old pro he is—at the age of nineteen.

"But it was then that the wheels began to come off for Billy Antrim. The getaway floater evidently simply wasn't there. Neither were any of his supposed colleagues. He was left stranded with the local sheriff's men coming in fast."

"Sheriff?"

"It's an old police term, going back to antiquity. They still use it in some areas. The head of the local commissariat of police. At any rate, Billy shot it out with them, killing one man and sending two to the medicos. He stole a floater and took off, apparently without plan."

"And he's remained at large all this time, on *Earth?*" Ronny said unbelievingly.

Sid Jakes held up a hand, grinning. "Wait. You haven't heard it all. The alarm went out, of course, and he was cornered again not three hours later." Jakes snorted. "This time he killed two men and wounded two bystanders, both women. Then he stole one of the police floaters and was off again. He ditched it later and at gun point forced three people out of a private floater and took off in it. But there was a pattern by now. They could see he was heading for Greater Washington, and set up road blocks."

By this time, Ronny was staring. The story was incredible.

"They flushed him twice more," Jakes said. "The last time, just last night. I don't think even the Old Man knows about this. I haven't taken it in to him yet. Two of the local floater patrol caught him in their bips and started in pursuit.

Mind you, this was a standard police floater, with all equipment. Evidently Billy realized he couldn't outrun them and lifted his vehicle to about a ten foot level and took out over the fields, with them after him. But it wasn't Billy's style to wait until they caught up and finished him off. No sir. He zipped around a corner, got out of his floater and waited. You can imagine their surprise when they came tearing around that corner and there was young Billy, waiting. By the way, he carries a gun that is at least as powerful as one of our Model H's. When we found the two patrolmen they were like tomato paste."

Ronny wound it up for the other. "So he made it to Greater Washington, and whatever his destination was."

Sid Jakes shook his head, as though pleased with the whole affair. "He has no destination. He's probably just trying to disappear into the city. Billy is basically a city boy, and it's the best place on Earth for him to hide. Don't think he'll head for the Palermo Embassy. He knows better. Billy Antrim hasn't survived this long by being stupid. He *knew*. He knew the moment that getaway floater didn't materialize that he'd been betrayed."

Sid Jakes leaned back in his chair, beaming at his subordinate. "So that's your phase of the job. Get Billy Antrim. I don't need to tell you what his continued freedom means to the department. If political assassinations can be successfully pulled off right here on Earth, heads are going to roll in Section G, starting with Ross Metaxa himself."

Ronny came thoughtfully to his feet. "How come we're not putting more men on it?"

Sid grinned at him. "Our prestige is low enough as is. If we assigned a dozen men to capture this callow boy, how would it look? Nope. There's only one of him, so there'll be only one Section G agent sent to get him. You'll have, of course, the support of all the police apparatus you'll need. Just call. But there'll be only one Section G agent."

He stood too and stuck out a hand for a shake. "It'll be a neat trick, if you pull it off, Ronny. And Ross'll have your scalp if you don't."

Ronny said acidly, "From what you say about this Billy Antrim, Ross'll never have a chance at my scalp if I foul up. Billy'll already have it."

XVI

BILLY ANTRIM WAS on the run under one of the most difficult situations conceivable.

He had no credit card acceptable on Earth.

Looking back at it now, he could see that Big Luigi had deliberately arranged that. The obvious thing would have been to have equipped Billy Antrim with several valid credit cards, just in case. Without one he could breathe and he could get water to drink, but practically all else was closed to him.

This was his first visit to Earth and his first contact with this type of exchange, but animal instinct told him that the simple stealing of a credit card wasn't the answer. At least, not a permanent answer. In an economy using this exchange medium, somewhere along the line would be ultra-efficient computors, checking and double-checking each transaction no matter how small. A stolen credit card might be used once or twice, but then whatever police powers were available to the accounting computors would be after the thief.

He slept the first night, his stomach empty, standing in the nearest equivalent he could find in the city of Greater Washington to a darkened alley. It was darkened through his own efforts, and he didn't like that bit of it, either. He had no way of knowing how soon the light failure would be taken care of by the city maintenance department. He slept standing, to the extent he slept at all, his hand never further than inches from the weapon in his belt, the gun which he knew how to use so well.

A maintenance squad floater came through at dawn and Billy, catlike, awoke fully from his drowze. He shrugged his shoulders in the nearest thing he had time for in way of stretching cramped muscles, gave his clothes a rapid brush, stuck his hands in his pockets and stepped out briskly, whistling a currently popular Palermo dance tune.

The two men of the squad looked at him blankly.

Billy grinned his toothy grin and said, "Sure is pretty this time of morning, ay? I just can't help comin' out and walkin' around."

One of the two men looked up at the lightening sky, his face still empty. Color was there. New color in the gray-black of night. He had seen dawn many thousands of times. Perhaps the first thousand had even awakened some feeling in him. Now, he wished he was in bed. The other one didn't bother to look up. He grunted sarcasm.

Billy, his hands still in his pockets, turned and went on his way, still whistling.

The first of the two looked after him for a moment. "Crazy young jerk," he muttered. "Doesn't know when he's well off. He'll freeze his bottom off in this weather with no more but that jacket on."

The other growled, "What the devil was he doing in this alley with the light off and all?"

The other grunted contempt of the question. "What d'ya think he was doing?"

Billy Antrim was going to have to eat. Already his head felt somewhat light as a result of having not eaten for . . . how long? There'd been two oranges and half a box of cookies in that floater he'd gloamed from those three scared-to-death yokes a couple of days ago. He sneered amusement. They'd thought he was on some juvenile romp and tried to give him their watches and jewelry. He needed three more watches like he needed a knife in the kidney.

But he had to have food.

The gods to whom Billy Antrim prayed when in his personal fox holes came through. The streets were still largely deserted, but immediately ahead of him a citizen lurched from a doorway and started up the avenue.

Billy's eyes darted around him. The streets were otherwise clear.

He called out, "Ay! Mac! you dropped somethun!"

The other swayed to a halt, reversed his engines and looked back at the hail. It could only have been for him. His lids were half lowered over cloudy eyes.

"Whuz the matter?" he slurred.

Billy came nearer. "I saw you drop somethun, just when you was coming out of that there house there."

The other fumbled hands over pockets, absently. "Oh," he said. Then, finally, "What?"

"I don't know what," Billy said plaintively. "I just saw you drop somethun, just when you were coming out of the lobby like."

The half-drunken, half asleep one grunted a sigh and started back for the door from which he had emerged. Billy followed him into the hall.

The drunk peered around. "I don't see noth—"

Billy clipped him over the back of the right ear expertly with the butt of the gun.

He couldn't safely leave him here. He couldn't even take the time to frisk him here. He grabbed the man by the collar of his jacket and hauled him slowly toward the back recesses of the hall. Given luck, he wouldn't be found until other inhabitants of the building issued forth later in the day. Especially if Billy did some more in the way of darkening lights.

He sent his hands briskly over the other's clothing. He was interested in nothing beyond the credit card, and found it without undue effort.

He stood and looked down at his victim. One of his tutors, Piero Caravaggio, of the Agrigento staff, had once told him that if you kicked an unconscious man in the side of the head a couple of times, he wasn't able to remember your description upon regaining consciousness. It sounded unlikely to Billy, but when you had only one chance in a million, you couldn't afford to ignore any opportunity to better your odds. He kicked twice.

Before the romp which had culminated in the elimination of Giorgio Schiavoni, Billy had spent a few days with some of the boys sampling the fleshpots of Greater Washington.

Thus it was that he was acquainted with the location of those areas of town which catered to the nightowl set, or the workers, theatrical and otherwise, which in any big city must be fed and ministered to at all hours. He summoned a copter-cab at the next corner, dialed the coordinates he wanted and took it to within several blocks of his destination. When the cab stopped, he hesitated. He could do one of two things: press his newly acquired credit card to the cab's payment screen, which would automatically open the door for him, or break the lock and escape. Which would, of course, immediately set the powers that be after him.

No, the safest thing was to use the card. The drunk he had rolled, with any luck at all, would still be unconscious. Would certainly not as yet have noticed the loss of his card. In fact, given the Antrim luck, the yoke probably would get himself home and into bed to sleep it all off, before discovering his loss. Even then, he would probably list it as lost, rather than stolen—given the Antrim luck.

Billy pressed his card to the cab's screen and dismounted from the vehicle, which took off into the traffic just beginning to materialize.

He went into a monstrously large cafeteria type restaurant which catered to actors, musicians and the like. He ate once and hugely for the sake of his stomach as it was. Then he went back and past the array of foods once again, this time selecting such items as fruit, bread rolls, sandwiches and cake, which he could carry with him, and returned with these items to his table, tucked away in a largely unoccupied cove of the dining room. There he wrapped them up in an abandoned theatrical publication he had found.

With his package under his arm, he went to the men's room and did all that was possible to erase the ravages of the past three days. He wasn't going to be able to be conspicuous on the streets. He had no illusions; every police authority on the planet Earth was on the lookout for Billy Antrim. Happily, his beard was so light as to be almost meaningless, which was a godsend, since he had no shaving facilities.

By the time he issued from the restaurant, it was fully day and he merged into the foot traffic on the pedestrian level of the street.

He had got no more than a block before whining sirens ululated behind him. He came to a shocked halt. This was *too* quick. The drunk should still be unconscious, still groggy enough not to realize his credit card had been lifted. But even if he had recovered, the fuzz-yokes shouldn't be on Billy *yet*.

An auto-department store had opened side doors for the entry of its few workers. Billy Antrim entered briskly, strode at the same speed as the others, went to the lifters and took one to the third floor. He went over to the windows and looked back the way he had come.

There were three floaters, obviously police floaters, pulled up before the restro-cafeteria from which he had emerged only moments before, and disgorging hurrying men, some in uniform. His lips were white over his prominent teeth in a wolf-grin.

Had he known it, Billy Antrim was at that moment looking at the back of his eventual Nemesis, the man who would send him to his death.

XVII

RONNY BRONSTON STRODE quickly into the interior of the restro-cafeteria, flanked by Lieutenant Rogozhsky of the Baltimore section of Greater Washington's police. Rogozhsky was highly sceptical.

Ronny said sharply, "Have your men go through the place. Thoroughly. Then take on the neighborhood. If he's not here, we've probably missed him, but possibly not. He probably needs clothes, a razor, that sort of thing. He might be in a nearby store."

Rogozhsky said sceptically, "You don't even know this is him. For that matter, you don't even know he's in the city."

Ronny Bronston flicked open a wallet container. The badge

inside said simply, *"Section G, Bureau of Investigation,"* and it gleamed with a silver sheen.

Ronny said flatly, "I am giving orders, Lieutenant, not debating opinions."

Lieutenant Rogozhsky flushed, came to the salute and muttered, "Yes, sir." He turned to his men and took out some of his feelings on them.

Ronny said, "We're police. Twenty minutes ago somebody here ate a fantastically large meal, then, on the same credit card, bought a great deal of picnic type food. Did you see him—or her?"

The manager was shaking his head. "This place's completely automated, Citizen . . . whoever you are. We aren't one of these swanky joints with waiters and all that jetsam. We don't specially notice nobody that comes in here. We only got four people on a shift. How'd you expect . . ."

Ronny said urgently, "A young fellow. Maybe twenty years old. He probably sat off by himself. He was possibly a little shabby in appearance. Even dirty. He probably finally left with a package under his arm—the extra food he'd bought. He probably spent quite a time in the wash room."

"Hey," the other exclaimed. "You're right. A young fella. He sat over there. Over in that corner. He was kind of rumpled up, like he maybe slept in his clothes. He went into the washroom and stayed there quite a time. Then when he went out he had this paper bundle under his arm."

"How long ago?" Ronny snapped.

"Hell, maybe five minutes before you come in!"

"Lieutenant!" Ronny yelled. "It's him! Get your men on the streets. Get your communicator for more floaters. He left no more than five minutes ago!"

Lieutenant Rogozhsky was a competent officer, no matter what his opinion might be in regard to Bureau of Investigation bigwigs interfering with his department's affairs. He got on the ball.

Ronny Bronston took a small communicator of his own from an inner pocket. It looked innocuously like a woman's vanity case. He sat down at a table, propped it before him and clicked it on.

He snapped to whoever was at the other end. "It's Antrim. We're no more than five minutes behind him. He's got himself a credit card somewhere. We'll check back on that later. I suspected he'd be desperately hungry and that the first time he ate it would be a gargantuan meal, followed by something he could take along. I had the computors watching for such an order. It came through. The credit card he's got is 25X-3342-K852-Division GW. Alert all computors to check every purchase on that card. Alert at least a thousand police floaters, all over the city. We're in the Baltimore area, but he might already have taken a pneumatic somewhere else. They're to be on instant alert for when he uses that card the next time."

Billy Antrim had intuition as well as cunning. He ditched the credit card in the first waste chute he passed and left the department store by a back entry.

He strode, seemingly at ease, hands in pockets again, and slouching like a high school youngster. But nonchalant though his pace seemed, he made the best time he could without looking as though he was in a hurry. Several police floaters, dashing about in high state of efficient confusion, passed him by, going this way, going that.

With his left hand he loosened the weapon in his belt. It was getting warm. Much too warm. They were bringing in every fuzz-yoke in the city.

He stopped at a traffic regulator and spoke to the occupant of a floater who was impatiently waiting a go-ahead.

Billy stuck his head in the window, grinned ruefully and said, "Ay, citizen, you goin' over toward the river?"

The citizen in question scowled at him. "What of it?"

"Well, I'll tell you. You'll probably just laugh but . . ."

The other grunted, darted a look at the regulator. He was still held up. It'd take more than some youngster's minor tragedy, whatever it was, to make him laugh this time. of day, especially since he hadn't even had time for coffee.

Billy was saying plaintively, ". . . so the fellas though it'd be a big joke to swipe my junior I.D. credit card. And when the party was over, here I am, and I can't even take a pneumatic."

"Okay, okay, climb in. I'm not going to cancel my dial, though. I'll take you as close as we get to wherever you're going. Then you'll have to manage however you can."

"Gosh, thanks a million, Citizen."

Billy climbed in, slouched down in the seat, teenage style, and watched city, traffic and pedestrians go by. The fuzz-yoke was getting thicker by the minute.

The floater swung up to a higher level for speed and Billy noted the passing of the town below with satisfaction. They'd have Baltimore behind them in moments.

His benefactor remained glumly silent, which was all right so far as Billy Antrim was concerned, until they reached the vicinity of the Potomac.

He said, then, "You said the river, boy. Where do you want me to drop you?"

Billy Antrim said softly, "You aren't dropping me, Mac. I'm dropping you."

The other blurted, "What's that supposed to mean?"

Billy brought the gun from his belt with an easy motion and held it on the other's waist. "This is a romp, Mac. Put the floater on manual, and let's get down."

"Why, you damn . . ." The other reached for him, in fury.

With a fluid speed, Billy slapped him hard against the side of the head with the gun barrel. Then he slugged him again, more deliberately, but more effectively.

Billy sneered. Once a yoke, always a yoke. It was like Big Luigi had always said. You never got over it. You're born a yoke and you die one.

He frowned at the thought. Who was he to be appreciating Luigi Agrigento? Luigi had treated him as though he was a yoke himself. Even as he was turning the floater controls to manual, Billy Antrim had the first twinge of doubt about the philosophy in which he had been raised. Maybe this citizen he had just slugged was only a yoke, but Billy wondered if he would have sent what amounted to a son to his sure death to gain only a minor advantage, a Maffeo revenge.

Fortunately, his victim was an even smaller man than was Billy Antrim. By considerable effort he was able to boost him over the front seat into the back and down on the floor of the vehicle. Billy then gave him another tap on the temple—with the butt of the gun this time.

He brought the vehicle to a near-stop and considered his situation. He was without a credit card again. He had one possibility that came to him immediately. He could lift this yoke's card, kill him rather than just leaving him unconscious, get out of the floater after dialing it to, say, Mexico City, and then have the use of the card for possibly as much as twenty-four hours before the floater and its body were discovered. The auto drive would take it clear through to Mexico, and tucked down on the floor like this, the yoke would probably never be spotted.

He didn't know why he decided against the step. Perhaps, for one thing, he wasn't sure he'd have the use of the card for that length of time. He couldn't figure out how the fuzzyoke had got onto him so quickly with that last credit card he'd stolen. There must be some angle he wasn't aware of.

He sneered self-deprecation and dialed the floater toward the Norfolk section of the city. It was about as far as he could get from where they'd flushed him in the Baltimore area, and besides, it was one of the oldest and least respectable sections of town—where the interplanetary spacemen hung out, and those that were this millennium's nearest equivalent to the slum elements of an earlier age. His clothes would attract less attention here.

When he put down, in as quiet a vicinity as he could find, he took up his bundle of food, slipped his newly acquired credit card into his pocket, slugged his benefactor once more for luck, and dialed the floater's controls to Richmond. After it had disappeared with its unconscious passenger, Billy faded into the neighborhood.

XVIII

RONNY BRONSTON WAS looking on the harassed side, and Sid Jakes' grin of derision didn't make him feel any the happier.

Ronny said, "He's got a new credit card. One that he got from an electrical engineer whose apartment is in the Baltimore area. A fellow named Ernest Gutenberg."

Sid flicked a switch. "What did you say the number was?"

"78Y-7634-L991 and, of course, Division GW."

"How do you know it was Antrim?"

"Who else? We were minutes behind him. Somehow he managed to get into Gutenberg's floater. The man's wife says that he was heading for his office, near the Capitol Building Museum. When he was found, on the floor of the back seat, his credit card was gone and the floater had come to a halt in the center of the Richmond area. By the way, Billy's score, here on Earth, has gone up to seven. Gutenberg died from concussion. Seven dead, half a dozen wounded in varying degree."

Sid Jakes nodded, his face grim for once. "The little rat is a one man task force." He bounced up from his chair, walked unhappily about his desk, sat down again. "Maybe we ought to put more men on it," he groused.

"No!" Ronny blurted.

Sid looked at him and chuckled. "Getting to be a matter of pride, eh? Where do you think he is?"

"Probably in the Norfolk area. He hasn't used his new card yet. That youngster's like a cornered fox. He hasn't done anything wrong yet . . ." Ronny Bronston took in the amused expression on his superior's face and growled. "I mean he hasn't done anything wrong from his viewpoint. With his luck, he should have become a gambler instead of a professional gun for hire."

"Why Norfolk?" Jakes said.

"It's the farthest point from Baltimore still in Greater

Washington. And, besides, it's a section where he can stay
the most inconspicuous. His clothes must be getting on the
crumby side by now, but there are others with crumby
clothes in Norfolk."

Sid said happily, "I'm glad it's your problem, instead of
mine. Where do you think he's hiding himself?"

Ronny didn't answer. He said, instead, "Look, can you
have Irene go to work on alerting every museum, every art
gallery, every library in Greater Washington? Every place
where entry is free and there are chairs, rest rooms and lots
of people. Same for parks, zoos, that sort of thing. Alert all
attendants at such places. Do we have a picture of him yet?"

"No." Jakes said. "Through our attaché in Palermo we've
picked up all the dope on him we can, but no picture as yet.
But we can have one of the artists do up a sketch based on
his physical description. Buckteeth, light brown, almost blond
hair, blue eyes."

"Okay," Ronny said wearily, coming to his feet. "I think I'll
get over to the Norfolk area. If I had to disappear in this city,
I think that's where I'd head."

Sid chuckled amusement. "From what we've seen of this
Billy Antrim, he's probably one ahead of you. He figures that
that's where you'd figure he'd be, so he's probably in some
swank area such as Arlington, or maybe back in Baltimore."

"You're great for my morale," Ronny muttered. "How's the
rest of the case going?"

Sid Jakes shook his head. "Stymied. Billy Antrim wasn't a
citizen of Palermo. The Palermo Embassy denies they had
anything to do with the shooting of Giorgio Schiavoni. Claim
it must have been a personal matter between Antrim and
Schiavoni. In fact, they hint there was bad blood between
the two, when Schiavoni and Billy were both back on Palermo. What's more, they're hinting rather heavily that even
in questioning them about the matter, Article One is being
strained, if not broken."

"Oh, swell," Ronny said.

"Worse than you think," Sid grinned. "Ross is going
drivel-happy. This is a real tough one. Most of the victims of

our Section G shenanigans never know what hit them. They're not looking for our particular type of double-dealing. Palermo's another thing. The Maffeo lads suspect *everybody*, given cause or not. Our representatives on their planet are bugged, shadowed, have their mail read and their space cables scanned, automatically."

"So what's the answer?" Ronny said.

"We don't have any answer. Not so far," Sid said, as though pleased. "The way it looks to me, Luigi Agrigento and his Maffeo are going to live happily ever after, and Palermo is going to remain in the dark ages, whether or not the balance of United Planets continues to haul its way up by the bootstraps."

Ronny Bronston said, "I'm glad I'm only a bloodhound on this assignment. You and Ross can have the headaches."

XIX

BILLY ANTRIM WAS in Norfolk, all right, but in one other respect he was one ahead of his unknown pursuer. He wasn't foolish enough to spend his time in museums, zoos, or even parks. His intuition as a killer animal on the run told him that such institutions would be on the watch.

Instead, he made his way to the nearest secondary school, slouched his way in in his now practiced imitation of the teenager of all centuries, joining the crowd. At the first opportunity, he took up a pile of books which some negligent student had left unsupervised for the moment, and carried them along under his arm in like fashion to his neighbors.

He located the school library and stayed there as long as he thought practical, and then managed to find the students' projection rooms, where he spent the rest of the morning watching educational Tri-D tapes. It didn't take him long to locate those pertaining to historical matters involving wars of the past and such items of violence.

He discovered by chance that noon-time meals in the

school's cafeteria were free and saved his paper wrapped reserves from the restro-cafeteria of that early morning.

But sleep was now becoming the ultimate necessity. He hadn't truly slept for three days and even youth has its limits, especially when under the stress being carried by Billy Antrim.

However, he couldn't discover a hiding place in the school buildings where he could trust himself for even an hour, and he knew that if he took the chance, an hour would never do. Once down, he was going to be a log for at least eight hours, possibly more. He couldn't afford to let down his defenses for that length of time, even if he had found a hole in which to hibernate.

The Antrim luck continued to hold when school let out. He took up his books and drifted along with the current of students, those who were pedestrian. He hated to be out in the light of day at all but at least he had protective coloring for a time. He had no idea of how good a description Earth authorities had of him. For all he knew, Luigi Agrigento might have even leaked them a photograph, his fingerprints and whatever else they might have wanted the better to hunt down Billy Antrim. His lips pulled further back in a wolf-like, humorless grin; Big Luigi wasn't going to be entirely happy until he got word that his former protégé was no more. There was a lot Billy knew about the workings of the Maffeo.

As his fellow students dropped off to the left and right, Billy Antrim was faced with the problem of new camouflage. He wasn't going to be able to walk the streets, certainly not after nightfall, with his armload of books and remain inconspicuous. He had to find shelter, and, above all, he had to find sleep.

He pulled up short before a Sauna-Turkish Bath.

If it was anything like the Moorish type bath which had come down in Sicily from the days when the Saracens had occupied that island, and later went on the planet Palermo . . .

He'd take the chance. He entered.

The place was, of course, highly automated. There was

but one attendant and he, bored, was scanning a portable Tri-D set. He hardly looked up. "In there," he said.

The dressing room had individual lockers, of course. Right now, he was the only customer. Billy Antrim hesitated only momentarily before parting with his clothes, his food supply and, above all, his knife and gun. But there was nothing for it. He locked them up and slid the elastic which bore the key about his wrist.

There were lettered instructions about the room. He followed directions, spent a minimum time in the steam room, took one quick plunge in the pool, then sought out the massage rooms. They were separate cubicles. He entered one. There was no key, but the door evidently registered OCCUPIED when someone was inside.

He sneered at the instructions for making operative the electrical masseur and flung himself down on the massage table, asleep before his body had completely relaxed on the hard surface.

A voice said, "Hey, chum, you fell asleep. You figuring on stayin' all night?" There was a laugh, as though something hugely amusing had been said.

Ordinarily, Billy Antrim's awakening was instantaneous, as a professional killer's should be. But now his exhausted body resisted awakening. He muttered something, fretfully.

"Come on, come on, boy. I'm closing up."

Billy Antrim felt a less than gentle hand shaking him. He came instantly alert, staring at the other, his blue eyes ice.

The attendant he had seen earlier in the other office pulled back his hand quickly. He said, stubbornly, "It's closing."

Billy swung his legs around and to the floor.

"Awright," he muttered. "Gosh, I musta fell asleep."

The attendant left and Billy made his way back to the dressing rooms and reacquired his belongings. Nothing had been touched.

This was the crucial point, now. Before returning to the entry office, he loosened the gun beneath his jacket, but then assumed a puzzled and repentant expression.

111

He approached the desk with its payment screen against which to press a credit card.

"Ay, Mac," he said sorrowfully. "Guess what? I'm sorry, but it looks like I forgot my credit card."

"Oh, yeah?" The attendant looked at him truculently. "I shoulda noticed. Why, you probably ain't even got a adult card. Come on, boy. Get that junior I.D. out. You're not talking yourself out of paying up. I seen dead beats before."

Billy said doggedly, "I'm sorry, Mac, but like I told you. I musta left it home. I'll pay you tomorrow."

"I never even seen you before. I'm calling the police, sonny. Nobody's walking out on this business." He reached for a switch.

Billy Antrim had two alternatives. The butt of the gun was within inches of his right hand. But a new killing would bring down the fuzz-yokes, and they were already too close behind for comfort.

He said hurriedly, "Look. This here ring. It's a star sapphire. I'll let you keep it, until tomorrow. Then I'll come back and pay off."

The other's eyes narrowed in greed. "Okay, boy. I trust you. You know how it is."

"Yeah, sure," Billy said bitterly. "I know how it is." He turned and left.

His mother had given him the ring. Back when they had been flush once. He suspected it had been given to her by a male admirer, most likely a lover, but it was the only thing he still possessed to keep alive the memory of Ruth Antrim, the one person he had ever loved. Now it was gone.

What had happened to Ruth Antrim? After Big Luigi had shipped her off, Billy had never heard. She had probably written him, she would have written, but he suspected Luigi Agrigento had confiscated any such mail. Luigi at the time was amusing himself by educating the boy in the traditions of the Maffeo, and in the use of the gun, the knife, the sap.

It was dark on the street. Warily, Billy Antrim trudged along, portraying the schoolboy who had dropped off at a theater and was now making his way on home.

PLANETARY AGENT X

He had no time to be thinking of Ruth Antrim and Luigi Agrigento, but for the moment he couldn't keep them from his mind. For the past three days fingers of doubt had been touching sensitive spots in his mind. While still a member of the Maffeo machine of Palermo, it had been easy enough to rationalize his way of life. The things he did were by order of Big Luigi himself, weren't they? And Luigi Agrigento was the most important man on Palermo. It was as simple as that. What Big Luigi said was law.

But now, as a victim of the machine, rather than a cog in it, the injustice of the Maffeo way was more evident.

Billy Antrim sneered at himself, in sour self-deprecation. He was a rat on the run. Why not face reality? He was scum that the decent members of the race had to mop up. And then, contradictorily, he told himself in braggadocio that they'd have their work cut out in the mopping.

"One chance in a million," he muttered.

It was getting too late for a schoolboy to be out. He'd be the more conspicuous by hanging onto the guise. He dropped the books into a waste disposal chute, straightened up and walked with a swagger, and as though he had already had two or three drinks before going out on the town seriously.

With luck, he decided, he might be able to crash a party. A party that would provide food and drink, though drink he could do without. Even at the most secure of times, a little alcohol went far with Billy Antrim. He could afford no blurred edges now.

He didn't find the party, but he did as well.

A middle-aged, slightly overweight, overly-blonde, overly-dressed madonna of the cocktail lounges allowed him to pick her up. In fact, she couldn't have been more obviously approachable had she dropped her handkerchief. She reminded him of someone, but he couldn't finger the resemblance.

In their early preliminaries, she giggled archly and said, "I must be robbing the cradle. Why, you can't . . ."

Billy was looking his most adult. "I know I look young.

113

Always have. I guess when I get up into my fifties, I'll be glad. Now it's a pain in the neck. Anyhow, I'm twenty-five. And I'll bet you're not any older."

She giggled again. "Well, to tell you the truth . . ."

"Call me Jimmy," he said.

"All right. I'm Betty Ann. To tell you the truth, Jimmy, I'm twenty-five too."

She was a good twenty years senior to that, Billy decided cynically.

"How about a drink?"

"We don't have to go any further than in there, Jimmy," she laughed, indicating the nearest auto-bar. "You know, I'm glad we met. I think we're going to have fun. Wasn't it a coincidence?"

It turned out that he had left his credit card at home.

She laughed at that, too. At the edge of forty-three, Betty Ann had picked up the bills before. She didn't particularly mind any more. Her need was for young men and to indulge it she had found long since that the best bet was to haunt the poorer sections of the city—and to be quick and willing to press her own credit card to the payment screen.

XX

HE SPENT the night at her apartment. Not that it did her much good. In spite of his youth, and what she had hoped would prove his prowess as a lover, it was as a deep sleeper that he turned out to be a veritable phenomenon. Betty Ann was disgusted.

In the morning she fed him breakfast, sitting across the breakfast nook from him, taking no more than coffee for herself.

In the light of day, without cosmetics, she was fully her age. Perhaps even a bit older in appearance than reality, for the past ten years had been hard ones, filled as they were with desperate attempt to halt the flight of youth in parties, in alcohol, in hard pursuit of Eros. It was all Billy could do to bring his eyes to her face, even as he wolfed a prodigious breakfast of six eggs, a full quart of milk, six or eight slices of bacon and as many of toast, with butter and marmalade.

He had placed who she reminded him of, now that he saw her in morning's unkindly light. Ruth Antrim. His mother after playing the late hour shows; tired and disheveled and caring nothing—except for him, of course.

Betty Ann watched him wearily as he ate. "What did you plan on doing today?" she said finally. There was no girlish giggle in her voice now, only the weariness of a middle-aged woman who wouldn't, who couldn't, quite give up as yet.

He looked up at her, quickly looked down again. "I don't know," he said. Then, slowly, "You're a lot of fun."

"No, I'm not," she said.

"Sure you are. Why don't we just hang around here today? It's my day off. We'll hang around and have a lot of laughs."

"And tonight you'd spend here again, eh?"

"Well, sure."

"I'm afraid not, Billy."

His eyes were blue ice. "The name's Jimmy."

"Kids named Jimmy don't carry guns with the front sight filed away and the forepart of the trigger guard, so as not to get in the way of a quick draw."

His voice was as level and cold as his eyes. "You seem to know a lot about guns, lady."

She shrugged, wearily. "I read a lot and watch the Tri-D shows a lot. A single woman my age has got lots of time to watch the shows. I woke earlier than you and watched this morning for awhile. The drawing they show of you isn't very good, but good enough, Billy Antrim."

He looked at her, poker-faced, but his mind was racing.

She shook her head. "If you had to be worried about me telling them, I could have done it hours ago. All I had to do was pick up the phone while you were still asleep, after I had checked your clothes and found the gun. I suppose I should have . . ."

115

"I don't like that kinda talk, Betty Ann."

". . . But I didn't. I don't know why. You'd better go now, though."

He looked at her for a long moment. He couldn't figure out why she hadn't called the police, either. She certainly wasn't in love with him; he wasn't the type to inspire love in a woman. Besides, she hadn't had time to fall in love with him. And be in love with a seven-time killer on the lam? Not even a woman as desperate as Betty Ann.

His best bet would be to add her to his list. She would have a better description of him than was evidently available thus far. She'd said the drawing they were showing over the air wasn't so good. She'd be able to improve it for them.

She chose that moment to reach for the coffee pot, wearily. He had seen Ruth Antrim in that exact pose a thousand times.

A thousand times back in those days when there had been only the two of them. And when all the world had been only the two of them. When no one else had counted. Tired she might have been, exhausted from twice the number of shows a performer should have been expected to give—but never so tired that she couldn't discuss the dream with him.

The dream of their settling down somewhere and of Ruth finding some other manner of supporting them—it had never been quite clear what that might be, since she had known nothing else but show business. And he would go to school, and soon, very soon, such would be his efforts, he would be able to find a grand position of his own, and then Ruth Antrim would need work no longer. And then, indeed, the goal would have been reached. A home of their own, with Ruth to keep it and with Billy faring forth each morning to his labors, and she there to greet him at day's end.

He more or less knew it now for a boy's dream and that of a tired woman in her early middle years. Deep within, he knew it had lacked reality. That at best there had been no room in it for his own marriage and eventual children. There had been no room in it for anything or anyone except Ruth and Billy Antrim. But still it was a dream that came back to him.

116

Billy Antrim didn't have many dreams.
He shook his head and came to his feet.
"Goodbye, Billy," Betty Ann said after him.

Ronny Bronston was saying into his portable communicator, "It was him, all right. The description tallied. He's evidently got Gutenberg's credit card, but is too smart to use it unless it's an emergency. He went into a Sauna-Turkish Bath in Norfolk and spent nearly four hours there. Sleeping, of course. Then he told the attendant he'd forgotten his credit card and left a star sapphire ring as a pledge."
Sid Jakes interrupted him quickly: "You think he'll go back to redeem it?"
Ronny snorted. "Of course not. I think he's cunning enough *never* to go back to where he's been before. Besides, he'd be in the same position as before. The moment he used the credit card, to redeem his ring, we'd be onto him. At any rate, the Sauna-Turkish Bath attendant had second thoughts about the ring, wondering if it was stolen. It seemed too valuable to have been left in lieu of such a minor amount. He reported it, and the police relayed the story to me. They relay anything that involves somebody getting or trying to get something, or some service, without having a credit card."
"You don't seem to be making much progress," Jakes chuckled, as though that was amusing. "Ross is beginning to have second thoughts about assigning you to the job."
Ronny grunted. "At least I know I was right, before. He's in the Norfolk area. And now, with his face all over town, he'll be doubly hard put to hide himself. He'll show. Within twenty-four hours I wager he'll show. His luck can't hold forever."

XXI

However, it was holding thus far.
Billy Antrim had to stay out of the light, and that was exactly what he was doing. In the cheapest part of the Nor-

folk section of Greater Washington, he was sitting, half sprawling, at a table in the darkest bar cum nightclub he could locate, the *Pleasure Palace*.

Had he dared, he would have put his face in his arms, as though in drunken sleep, but he was afraid that the one caustic faced usher who supervised the automated alleged amusement center would have ordered him from the premises. As it was, he leaned his face on a cupped hand, so that the fingers could cover his prominent teeth, his chin and part of the nose, and pretended to watch the fairly spicy canned Tri-D show.

He had to do something, and fast. As it was, the only thing he was accomplishing was to keep a few jumps ahead of the authorities. He knew it was only a few jumps by the inordinate number of police floaters on the streets. It had been nip and tuck a few times. They obviously knew he was in the Norfolk area. He had to do better than this, or it was just a matter of time before he slipped and they would have him.

At the thought of it, he loosened the gun. He would at least go out with a bang. He twisted his mouth at the thought. He undoubtedly would, but what would be accomplished? What percentage was there in his being able to take two or three more of the fuzz-yokes with him—or even a hundred more?

The usher was eyeing him.

Billy had sat down at a table where there were a couple of glasses, one of them with an inch of dregs still in the bottom. He had pretended this glass was his own, but even had the usher been fooled on that—his eyes hadn't been on Billy when he'd entered—he had evidently gotten around to noticing that his new customer wasn't doing much in the way of drinking up and dialing anew.

He had to do something, or leave. If the usher got around to coming to the table, he might recognize the Antrim features, even in this light.

Billy got to his feet and stepped over to the next table, which was occupied by a single customer, obviously deep in his cups. He couldn't have been much more than in his early twent es himself, surly faced, soft in spite of his age, a trickle of drink-induced saliva at the side of his mouth. He was sloppy drunk.

"Ay," Billy said, grinning, "ain't you Steve Osterman, met at a party last week?"

The other glowered up at him. "No, I ain't no Steve whatever. And we never met at no party."

Billy shook his head in wonder and slid into a chair at the other's table. "Well, we sure as hell met somewheres. I never forget a face."

The other grunted. "Name's Barry. Horace Barrymore. Ev'body calls me Barry."

Billy snapped his fingers. "That's it. Barry. Now I remember. It was a great party."

The other scowled at him. "You from Detroit too?"

"Sure. Of course. That's where the party was. What you doing in Greater Washington, Barry?"

The other squinted at him slyly. "Gotcha that time. I never been in Detroit. I'm from Miami-Havana, see? And I got you figured out, Buster."

Billy's hand dropped into his lap. "Oh, you have, eh?"

"Yeah. I know you, Buster." The other chuckled to himself and picked up his glass. It was empty.

From the side of his eyes, Billy Antrim could see the usher making his way in their direction.

The self-named Barry grinned. "Yep. You're a drink cadger. Thas what. You just kinda pretend you know a guy and get talkin' to him, hopin' he'll spring for a drink. Well, Buster, let me tell you somethin' . . ." He hesitated for a long moment, as though having dropped his trend of thought. "Let me tell you somethin'." He burped. "Let me tell you, you picked the right man, Buster. I'll buy you a drink. Fact, I'll buy you a whole flock of drinks."

Billy let air out of his lungs, silently.

The other punched the auto-controls. "Pseudo-whisky and wasser, eh? Man's drink. And where I'm goin' there's nothin' but men needed."

119

The drinks appeared and the usher sheered off and headed elsewhere.

Billy said, cautiously, hiding his face behind the glass. "You celebrating somethun', Barry?"

"Damn right. I'm killing two birds with one stone, see? Two birds." For a moment he seemed to have lost his trend again. But then he said, "Spending my credit, see? No good where I'm going. And same time, celebratin' leavin' this damn Earth."

Billy said, keeping the conversation going, "You a spaceman?" He was wondering how best to approach his heaven-sent gift about ordering some food instead of more drink. The man might even have a hotel room he could be coaxed into sharing for the night.

"Spaceman!" the other sneered. "Do I look like a space rat? I'm a *colonist*. Par . . . part . . . participatin' in foundin' of a new worl'. Unnerstan'? Like the brochures said. Out into the glor . . . glorious far beyon'. Leave this stinkin' Earth behine. A man don't hava chance here. Never get anywhere. That right . . . whus your name? Have 'nother drink. I know you're nothin' but . . . spunger. But thas all right. Havanother drink."

"Make mine light ale, this time," Billy said softly. "Look Barry, you interest me, like. How you go around gettin' to be a colonist?" He ran his tongue over the bottom of his upper teeth.

The other grunted surly amusement, and rubbed thumb and forefinger together. "You inherit some ol' family art objects and convert 'em to credit. Thas how. Then you join up."

"Join up what?" Billy said softly. His blue eyes were only slits now.

The other was impatient at his stupidity. "Join up one of the companies, course. Put up your share. Join company. Pioneers. Out inta glorious far beyon'. Start up new worl'. Plenty chances for everybody. Live glorious natural life of frontiersmen of old. Get rich, exploitin' new worl'."

Billy Antrim said the next very softly. "Teamed up with a lot of your friends, eh?"

120

"Frens, hell. None of my frens ever had 'nough credit to make colonist. I just bough inta one of the new formin' companies. You gotta belong to a company, with lotta pull. Get permission to leave stinkin' ol' Earth. Gotta have pull ina high place. New Arizona Company. Hire a spaceship from Space Freightways. Land on New Arizona. Stake out claims. Live glorious natural life. Chance for everybody getta head. Not like stinkin' Earth—everybody down on you, less you benta lots school an' all."

The man was drooling drunk, Billy realized. Drunk beyond the point of memory tomorrow. He said, urging in his voice. "So you don't know anybody else among the colonists, ay? When do you check in with them?"

Barry eyed him owlishly, and for a moment Billy Antrim was afraid the other was going to fall forward, passed out. But with a dull shake of the head, he evidently regained enough clarity to get out, "Big party tonight. Spend all last Earth credits. Tomorrow, ev'thing set. Take shuttle rocket, local spaceport, shuttle out New Albuquerque. Got alla tickets. Get aboard S/S *Ley*. An' we burn off for New Arizona. Burn off. Thas space talk for . . ."

A voice from behind him said, "Friend, your buddy here seems to have had enough. In fact, I should've noticed him earlier. How about getting him on home?"

Billy, keeping his face averted, said, "Yeah. Suppose you're right, Mac."

The usher said, "Here, I'll help you with him. Cheese, he's really got a load on."

"Hey," Barry protested feebly. "I ain't drunk. I been drunker'n this. Big blowout. Gotta celebrate."

"Sure, sure," Billy soothed him. "Come on, let's get on home."

"Hey, wait up just a minute, friend. Somebody trot out his credit card. You got a man-sized bill here."

Billy moistened his lips. "The drinks were on him."

"Yeah. Well, by the looks of your pal, he's passed out. How about that? Hey, haven't I seen you someplace before?"

Billy said quickly, "I'll take care of it." He fished his purloined credit card from his wallet and pressed it against the payment screen. "Come on, help me to a cab with him. I wouldn't want him to puke all over your floor."

"Cheese," the other said. "Let's get going."

XXII

Ronny Bronston took the message in the police floater in which he was prowling the Norfolk waterfront entertainment area.

Credit Card 78Y-7634-L991-*Division* GW *has been utilized to pay a nightclub bill at the* Pleasure Palace. . . .

Ronny snapped to his driver, "You know where the *Pleasure Palace* is?"

"We passed it not five minutes ago. There on . . ."

"Get there! Fast!"

While the floater spun, ignoring traffic, narrowly averting disaster three times in thirty seconds, Ronny grabbed the hand mike.

"He's on the run! *Pleasure Palace* nightclub, Norfolk Waterfront. All floaters zero in! Something important happened. He's had to use the credit card. Zero in!"

Billy Antrim was as near to being in a funk as Billy Antrim ever allowed himself to get. He could hear the whining of the sirens from afar, a multitude of sirens. It brought to mind a faintest memory of youth when he had still been with his mother and their way of life had involved planet jumping with the troupe with which she had performed. It had been a planet in the Aldeberan group, he couldn't remember exactly which one. He'd been too young, but the planetwide holiday had been celebrated in a fantastic blowing of whistles and sirens. Thousands and thousands of sirens. On business buildings, on official cars, on factories, on ships, seemingly everywhere. It had been ear piercing, nerve racking . . .

He tore his mind from such nonessentials. He was in the

clutch now. It was no time to be thinking of Ruth Antrim, and childhood. He had to get out of here, but fast!

He had dialed the cab more or less at random. He hadn't the vaguest idea where this Horace Barrymore might be staying. Some hotel, undoubtedly, but which was a mystery.

A floater was screaming down the street at them. Billy dropped to the cab's floor, leaving his semi-conscious companion propped against the glass of the door, eyes bleary but open. A light flashed, lingered a moment on the other's face, then the police vehicle was past.

Billy Antrim muttered, "One chance in a million," and regained his seat.

Even as they sped, he went through the other's things. Ticket on the rocket shuttle to New Alburquerque. A small sheaf of papers identifying Horace Barrymore as a member of the New Arizona Company. A spaceport pass, signed by an official of the company and the first officer of the Spaceship *Ley*. And the credit card which would have made so much difference, had Billy been able to utilize it earlier to pay the bar bill at the *Pleasure Palace*.

But things were still looking up better than they had ever since the debacle that had taken place on the shooting of Giorgio Schiavoni. If he could only get out of this immediate tight spot.

Another floater was screaming up the sub-freeway toward them, its lights blazing. Billy ducked to the floor again. It was past.

His lips, white, thinned back over his prominent teeth in his wolf grin. As long as the fuzz-yokes were heading in the direction of the *Pleasure Palace*, he was comparatively safe. But as soon as the usher there revealed that Billy had left in a cab with a companion who was dead drunk, then the fat would be in the fire. They'd know what they were looking for.

Suddenly inspiration came. He grabbed up a directory, thumbed through it. Then quickly redialed the cab.

The auto-motel was only a few hundred yards away. The cab pulled up. As usual, there was but one clerk.

Billy got out and said, "Ay Mac, my buddy here took on too big a load. Gotta room?"

The clerk had seen drunks before. In his time he had seen literally thousands of drunks. Drunks no longer interested him in the slightest. "He got a credit card to register with?"

"Sure, here it is."

"You registering too?"

"Naw, just my buddy. Wait'll I dismiss this here cab." Billy manhandled Barry from the floater-cab, turned him over to the clerk to balance waveringly for the moment necessary to press the Horace Barrymore credit card to the payment screen, then turned back.

Between them, they managed to usher, push, half carry the flopping drunk to a room. Billy let him drop to a bed. He grinned at the clerk.

"I'll see he gets into the bed, and all. How about lettin' me have a bottle of pseudo?"

The other looked at him. "Ain't you guys had enough liquor?"

Billy chuckled deprecation. "Ernie here has, but not me. I only had one or two. Besides, when he wakes up tomorrow, he's gonna need a couple quick ones to keep him from dying. That's the way he handles it. Hair of the dog."

The clerk shrugged. "Each man can go to hell in his own way, I always say. I'll get the pseudo."

Billy began taking off the drunken Horace Barrymore's shoes. His mind, behind his poker mask, was racing. He had to handle this exactly right. He couldn't afford any mistakes now. On the road outside he could hear the floaters screaming by.

It was one chance in a million. Whoever was in overall command would expect—Billy was gambling—for the quarry to put as much distance between himself and the *Pleasure Palace* as possible. Instead, Billy had gone into hiding less than half a mile from the alleged palace of pleasure.

The pseudo-whisky came, the clerk gave another listless look at the drunk sprawled on the bed, grunted and left.

Billy Antrim had already taken the vital papers of the other. Now he stared down at him.

The spaceship left tomorrow.

Once spaceborne, he would be outside the jurisdiction of Earth. The ship wasn't even scheduled to set down on a United Planets world. It was colonizing a new planet. Billy Antrim would be answerable only to whatever authorities the colonists would set up. And Billy was going to be an invaluable citizen, so far as such authority was concerned. A new world, a frontier world, could use citizens with Billy's qualifications.

He turned his right hand over so that it was palm upward and gave it a flick. A double edged fighting knife slid into his grip.

He could put a sign on the door requesting that the room not be disturbed. He could leave a call with the auto-service to the same effect. It would be well into tomorrow afternoon before Horace Barrymore was discovered.

By that time Billy Antrim would be well on his way to the stars. And who knew what he would find out there? Perhaps the chance at a new life. A different life than the one Luigi Agrigento had decreed for him when he'd been a boy of eleven. A life not composed of gun and stiletto. A life with meaning, such as his mother and he had once dreamed of for him.

The thought went through his mind. Perhaps he might even meet Ruth Antrim out there, once again. It was only seven or eight years, after all. But then he sneered self-deprecation, even as he stepped toward the unconscious Barrymore, the knife blade gleaming. Seven years, but look what he had managed to become. Would Ruth Antrim want to see what he was today, or would he want her to?

There was a line slowly trailing into the huge passenger-freighter—reminiscent, somewhat, of Noah's animals trailing into the Ark. Indeed, most were filing along two by two. Billy Antrim was one of the few who were single. That was just as well, he told himself. Married couples were conservative, lacking aggressiveness, compared to a single man. Billy would be able to make his place in this New Arizona.

They gave you a shot here. A little bit further on, they asked some questions. Further on they checked your papers, and still later, you had to sign some things. Then you shuffled along again.

Toward the end, there were two burly ship's officers. Before Billy realized what they were about, they had touched him here, there, the places a man carries a gun. A quick frisk.

He started to protest, but the senior of the two grinned at him and whipped the gun from his belt.

"Sonny," he said, "in spite of all you've heard about adventure in space, it's not like that at all. Sorry. Captain's orders. No weapons among the passengers so long as we're spaceborne. You'll get this oversized cannon back when you land." He looked at it and grunted. "Where'd you get this thing, anyway?"

"It usta belong to my old man," Billy said sourly. "He usta be a gun crank, like."

"He must have been," the other chuckled. "Hey, Bob, look at this. Front sight filed away, and all."

But his companion had taken on the next colonist in the line.

Billy shuffled on toward the ship. He had carried the last hurdle.

There had been some crucial moments during the past twelve hours, but he had cleared every obstacle. He had crossed Greater Washington in another cab, using Horace Barrymore's credit card. He had got through the press of people at the shuttle-spaceport, without exposure, hiding his face in a handkerchief and sneezing time after time, just as he'd passed the ticket gate. He had sat in the back of the shuttle rocket, hiding his head in his arm and pretending sleep every time someone had come near.

Once outside Greater Washington, he felt some relief. He assumed they had circulated the inadequate drawing of him throughout the globe. Most likely. He didn't know. But at least people weren't *expecting* to run into him out here.

His papers had been cleared without difficulty. He had, on the rocket shuttle, practiced Horace Barrymore's shaky signature a few times. It wasn't difficult. A scribble.

It had carried him past, easily enough.

And now he was actually entering the ship.

At the entry level stood another ship's officer, sheaf of papers in hand.

"Name?"

"Horace Barrymore."

"Horace Barrymore. Here it is. Berth 33, Compartment Twelve. Down that way, son."

Billy Antrim went as indicated. He had no baggage, but on the other hand, neither did most of the others. The baggage had been checked earlier. Billy, of course, had none to check. After they were spaceborne he would put up a big howl, to cover. He could claim that they'd lost his things. It shouldn't be difficult. He might even get some sort of reimbursement.

Compartment Twelve was but a hundred feet or so down the corridor along which he walked. The door was closed. He opened it and stepped in.

Billy Antrim scowled. It didn't look to be the type of compartment devoted to passengers. On the far side of the room was a desk at which was seated an easy-going looking young man, his face tired and his clothing rumpled and dirty—like Billy himself.

He looked up quizzically. "Hello, Billy," he said, his hand reaching for the automatic which lay on the desk.

Billy Antrim blurred into motion. He crouched, his right hand flicked and the knife was there magically. He threw the hand back for the cast.

Ronny Bronston's eyes blinked in surprised alarm—his fingers were still inches from the gun.

Then there was something in the wild blue eyes of Billy Antrim. He threw the knife—

His throw was not quite true. It missed Ronny Bronston's

head by scant millimeters and broke its point in a clang on the steel bulkhead beyond.

The gun was trained on Billy's stomach.

The Section G agent took a deep breath, swallowed, then managed to say, "You missed, Billy. I didn't expect you to miss."

Billy Antrim sneered. "It's all luck," he said. "Everything's luck. I had one chance in a million, and didn't make it."

The gun was steady.

"Sit down over there, Billy. I set this whole thing up only minutes ago. I didn't expect you quite yet. But shortly there'll be some local agents of my department showing up. Then we'll get about our business."

Billy sat, his strained juvenile face still in sneer. "You ain't got a jug could hold me, yoke."

Ronny Bronston looked at him meditatively. Evidently the other didn't know that there were no prisons for such as him on presentday Earth. Criminals of Billy Antrim's ilk were turned over to medical science for rehabilitation.

Ronny said, "It's been a long trek, Billy. I don't mind admitting you almost made it. You know what your big mistake was?"

"Yes."

"Oh?" Bronston raised eyebrows.

"I didn't slit that drunken bum's throat last night. I should've. But instead I just poured more liquor down his gullet. I thought he'd stay under long enough for me to make it. He musta woke up right after I left."

Ronny Bronston looked at him in puzzlement.

"It doesn't sound like a man with your background. Why couldn't you kill him? You'd already finished off eight others."

"Seven," Billy muttered.

"Eight. One of those two women bystanders you wounded in Scranton died in the hospital."

Billy winced.

"With a record like that," Bronston pursued, "you should

have been capable of finishing Barrymore off to make sure
your back trail was clean."

Billy said sourly, "What difference does it make? Maybe
I was gettin' tired of all the killin'. Ever since I knew Big
Luigi give it to me, I been thinking about it all. About my
old lady, and how she always said I was gonna go to school
and all. But after I knifed one of Big Luigi's goons he sent
her off the planet, and I never seen her again."

For a long moment, Ronny Bronston looked at the other.
Billy Antrim, defeated now and at bay, still looked like nothing so much as a defiant school youngster, caught in some
misdemeanor and hauled before the principal. There was
even somewhat of a wistful quality in the juvenile killer's
face, as though of a child grown almost to adulthood who
had been allowed down through the years to press his face
against the windowpane and look in at the others, celebrating
their Christmases and birthdays—but never allowed to enter
and participate.

Ronny shook his head, as though to clear away a trend of
thought he couldn't afford.

He said, "I'm afraid not. I've been looking further into
your dossier, Billy. Section G has been checking you on
every planet you've ever set down on. And we've been checking that of Luigi Agrigento, too."

Billy was scowling at him. "I don't know what you're
talking about, ya stupid yoke. I know what happened to my
old lady."

"That's not Luigi Agrigento's way. His henchman molested
your mother and as a result you killed him. Somebody, given
Maffeo outlook, had to pay. And since it was your mother
who was the original . . ."

Billy Antrim was on his feet, shaking. "You *lie!*"

Bronston, his eyes wary, shook his head. "Sit down, Billy.
You know better. I have no reason to lie."

Billy slumped back into the chair, his once poker face
twitching. "You lie," he muttered.

Bronston shrugged, as though he couldn't care less. "Agrigento evidently turned her over to his goon's relatives. And

129

they . . . I didn't understand this part of it. What does *capontina* mean?"

"No," Billy Antrim whispered, his head in his hands, his body swaying. "*No.*"

Bronston said, an element of contempt in his voice. "You fizzled out, in the real clutch, Billy. You should have finished off Barrymore. And just a few minutes ago. You missed me with that knife on purpose, didn't you?"

Billy Antrim didn't answer.

"You haven't got the guts to kill any more, Billy," Bronston told him.

Irene Kasansky looked up from her screens and order boxes, her switches and buttons, and said with as near to a smile as Irene Kasansky ever came to a smile, "Hello, Ronny. How'd you make out in New Albuquerque?"

Ronny said, exhaustion in his voice, "Not now, Irene. Is the Old Man available?"

Irene snorted and said, "Sid Jakes is with him. But it's nothing more important than your report. Where've you been?"

Ronny didn't answer. He was too exhausted to go through this more than once. He pushed his way through the door to the back and headed for Ross Metaxa's office.

Sid Jakes was sitting in a heavy chair across from the commissioner, who sat behind his desk. They both looked up when Ronny entered without knocking.

He slumped into a chair.

"Ronny!" Sid chortled. "How come no reports? For awhile you had me worried. I was afraid our Billy-boy had done you in."

Ronny shook his head. "I haven't been in a bed for four days," he said.

Ross Metaxa reached down into his desk drawer and came out with his brown bottle. "Drink?"

"I guess so," Ronny muttered. "Even that stuff."

While Metaxa poured, Sid chuckled, "Well, I suppose the fact you're here winds up the Billy Antrim segment of our troubles with Palermo. Now we'll have to get to work on the basic problem of our Maffeo friends. And that's going to be a neat trick, if possible at all, what with Article One of the Charter."

Ross Metaxa handed the drink over to his field man and growled, "Did you have to finish him off, or were you able to capture him? He might turn evidence, in case we ever have anything to take into the interplanetary courts. But above all, it's good propaganda, the civilization bit. The fact that here on Earth we don't execute or even imprison criminals, not even murderers. We rehabilitate them and release them as valuable members of society. Gives a good example to rawer worlds."

Ronny shook his head. "Not exactly either. I've spent the last day and a half with Billy Antrim getting plastic surgery up in New Chicago."

"Plastic surgery!" Metaxa exclaimed, his moist eyes bugging.

Ronny knocked back the drink and shuddered. It was every bit as bad as he remembered it.

He said, "By the way, what ever happened to Ruth Antrim, Billy's mother?"

"What's that got to do with it? Have you gone completely crazy?" Ross was blurting.

Sid Jakes said, "We even traced that out. She's living on Goshen now. Married to some sort of mining engineer." He grinned. "I suspect you have another bomb to drop, Ronny."

"The Department of Dirty Tricks," Ronny muttered, unhappily. "You see, I had to goose Billy."

Ross Metaxa rasped, "Where's Antrim, damn it!"

Ronny Bronston looked at him. "On his way back to Palermo."

Even Jakes lost his poise at that one.

Ronny said softly, "He has a date with Luigi Agrigento."

Metaxa closed his eyes and talked as though to himself. "I can fire him. I can claim he went off his rocker. I know what he had in mind. He figured that one man murder mill will get Agrigento. But does the fool realize that if he doesn't and it comes out that the Bureau of Investigation had a hand in the attempted assassination of a Chief of State what it will mean? The member planets will drop out of UP like dandruff."

Ronny was shaking his head. He reached over, took the brown bottle and poured himself another. "Billy's familiar with Luigi's security. He'll be able to get through, especially with the plastic surgery. And remember, Billy is a citizen of Delos, not Palermo. The moment Luigi Agrigento dies by the hand of a citizen of another world, Article Two goes into effect. Palermo has been interfered with politically by another member planet of UP."

Ronny got to his feet, preparatory to leaving. His voice was dead. "Which will be an excellent excuse for the United Planets Space Force landing, and, uh, reestablishing order."

Sid Jakes, his face empty, said, "Antrim. You think he'll . . . ?" His voice dribbled off.

Ronny said flatly, "Get away? Not on Palermo. He's expendable. He was the tool Section G needed, and I used him." He grunted deprecation. "Remember when you told me how the guts of my conscience were going to be strained the first time I got one of the jobs we're really here for? I didn't know what you were talking about then. I do now."

Ross Metaxa scowled down at his brown bottle, wordlessly.

Nor did Sid Jakes say anything further.

Ronny said, "And now I think I'll go home and get drunk a little, and tell myself that the end justifies the means—though there hasn't been a decent thinker in the history of man who could arrive at that conclusion."

It was in a far place from the office of Ross Metaxa in the Octagon.

A slight figure was inching its way along a building ledge, his back and arms pressed tight against the stonework. He had about four inches upon which to operate. It was a matter of twenty or thirty yards, but he had few doubts.

"One chance in a million," he muttered. You didn't have

much better odds than that when your goal was one of the most highly protected Chiefs of State in United Planets.

However, he had his own gods and now he was praying to them, and they weren't going to turn him down.

They didn't.

He made it to the window, brought the gun from his belt and rested it on the window sill.

He said softly, "Big Luigi."

The heavy man behind the desk stiffened, startled, but didn't turn. For the moment he was frozen.

The voice came ever so softly, "You wouldn't remember the face, Luigi, but it's me, Billy Antrim. You remember. Billy, the kid you sent for Giorgi, down on Earth. I just wanted you to know, Luigi."

The heavyset man's hands flew—one to a button, one to a desk drawer.

Billy Antrim pressed the trigger, in an affectionate way.

And the guards stormed through the door, weapons in hand. Far too late for Luigi, but with ample time for Billy. For once again it was a matter of no getaway arranged for pistolero Billy Antrim.